OFFSIDE!

OFFSIDE!

Sandra Diersch

James Lorimer & Company Ltd., Publishers
Toronto

James Lorimer & Company Ltd., Publishers acknowledges the support
of the Ontario Arts Council. We acknowledge the financial support of the
Government of Canada through the Canada Book Fund for our publishing
activities. We acknowledge the support of the Canada Council for the Arts
which last year invested $20.1 million in writing and publishing throughout
Canada. We acknowledge the Government of Ontario through the Ontario
Media Development Corporation's Ontario Book Initiative.

Cover Image: iStockphoto

Library and Archives Canada Cataloguing in Publication

Diersch, Sandra
    Offside! / Sandra Diersch.

(Sports stories)
Also issued in electronic format.
ISBN 978-1-55277-851-7

    I. Title. II. Series: Sports stories (Toronto, Ont.)

PS8557.I385O33 2011   jC813'.54   C2011-902028-9

James Lorimer & Company Ltd.,   Distributed in the United States by:
Publishers   Orca Book Publishers
317 Adelaide St. West   P.O. Box 468
Suite 1002   Custer, WA USA
Toronto, ON, Canada   98240-0468
M5V 1P9
www.lorimer.ca

Printed and bound in Canada.
Manufactured by Friesens Corporation in Altona, Manitoba, Canada in July 2011.
Job # 99768

For my father,
who knows all about
being a dad.

CONTENTS

1 A FEW FLURRIES

The ground was rock hard. Several days of frost had frozen the mud on the playing field to an icy firmness. The members of the Vancouver Burrards soccer team were doing their best to keep upright. Already their goalkeeper, Stacie Hutchins, had a nasty bruise on her elbow from an earlier fall. To make things worse, the clouds had rolled in, thick and dark, threatening the girls down below.

"You know, the only person I ever met who actually enjoyed playing in this kind of weather was Annie. The rest of us just suffer in silence. Do I still have ten fingers?" Allison whispered to Alecia. She held out her hands, a worried frown on her face.

"Yeah, ten of them. Tuck them under your armpits. Mom says that's one of the warmest places on your body," Alecia suggested. This was their first game since the Christmas lull and they were all a little out of the habit of playing in the cold. The weather had been uncharacteristically cold for Vancouver, even if it was early January.

"It's kind of hard to run with your hands in your armpits, don't you think?"

"Hey, it was just a suggestion. Do you think it will snow?" Alecia asked as the two girls made their way across the field. She glanced up at the stormy sky, frowning. That winter, Vancouver had already been struck with a snowfall that had closed schools, shut down power, and wreaked havoc on the highways and bridges. Still, Alecia loved the snow. She was always fiercely jealous when her pen pal in Ottawa sent her pictures of the huge drifts of snow that fell there.

"It's going to do something," Allison muttered, taking her position. "But right now I just want to finish this game and go home and get warm."

The Burrards' centre and captain, Laurie Chen, won the toss and started the second half with a quick pass to Allison on her right. Allison moved through the Spitfires' end, controlling the ball with steely determination. The Burrards were down by a goal at the start of the second half. Since the season began five months ago, they had lost only two games — one against their longtime rivals, the Rocketeers, and one in the tournament in November, where they had placed second. Laurie had given them a stern pep talk during halftime.

"Remember the deal we made before Christmas?" she asked them. "We're having our best season ever and we're going to go out with the league's best win/loss ratio ever. That means we can't lose more than two games the rest of the season. We're only down by one. Let's focus and take this! Let's mow 'em down!"

Laurie's words ran through Alecia's head as she caught a pass and ran down the field, avoiding two Spitfire defenders. Her quick glance around the field found Rianne open and Alecia passed the ball just as she was tackled by a Spitfire forward. Rianne fell hard passing the ball to Allison and got up slowly, rubbing her thigh, her face a grimace. But in another second she was cheering as Allison sent the ball flying past the goalkeeper and into the net. The score was tied.

"Way to go, team!" their coach, Jeremy, called from the sidelines. "Keep it up! Play hard, keep up the pressure!"

Laurie got the ball to Allison, who passed to Alecia, but Alecia's return pass was intercepted and the play turned over. The Spitfire forward outworked the Burrard defence and moved dangerously close to Stacie. Allison charged her but missed the ball, and the Spitfire turned and got away from her. The girl passed to the Spitfire centre, who was challenged by Laurie. Laurie came up with the ball, but only briefly, before it was stolen by another Spitfire forward.

The Burrards couldn't seem to get the ball out of their own end and Alecia was getting frustrated. Had these girls been fed vitamins during halftime or something? she wondered, struggling to keep up as the ball passed from player to player, always dangerously close to Stacie. Allison finally managed to get possession and moved back up the field toward the centre line, but Alecia, in her eagerness to receive Allison's pass, went in offside. The whistle blew and play returned to the Burrards' end for a throw in.

"Keep it together, Burrards!" Laurie called, looking around at the group. "Still got lots of time to win this thing."

Alecia took a deep breath and let it out slowly. Concentrate, she told herself sternly. Focus on the play. She found her opponent and took up her position right beside her, jostling elbows with her as she waited for the ball to be thrown into play. It was picked up by a Spitfire, who dribbled a little ways toward the centre line then turned and passed to an advancing forward. Laurie managed to throw the girl off the ball but before Laurie could get control of it, it was picked off by another Spitfire and kicked toward the net. Marnie and Rianne stayed in close to Stacie, protecting the goal as the Spitfires tried to set up a shot. Allison and Laurie continuously managed to break up passes and get the ball away from the net only to have it brought back in. Finally the ball was forced out of bounds and the whistle blew, stopping play.

Jeremy called a much-needed time out and the girls ran to the bench. "You're keeping good pressure on them, but they're still outworking you," he said as they huddled around him, as much for warmth as to hear his words. "Think of the drills we've done in practice. You've got to fool them into thinking you're doing one thing and then do another. Feign right and go left, then grab the ball. Don't be outplayed by girls younger and smaller than you. Play smarter." He looked at them all for a second, letting them take in his words, then he made a couple of line changes and sent them back out onto the field.

The Burrards' forward managed to come up with the ball almost immediately and quickly got it out over the centre line and out of danger. She passed to Laurie, who carried it deep into Spitfire territory. Her pass to Nancy was picked off, but Laurie quickly regained possession and sent the ball to the Burrard forward waiting near the net. She feigned right, then kicked the ball to the left of the sprawling goalkeeper, giving the Burrards the lead.

There were still twenty minutes of play left and the Spitfires continued with their aggressive checking and drives up the middle. It seemed to the Burrards that their goal must have been a fluke because the ball barely left their own end for the rest of the game. Finally, however, the referee blew the whistle ending the game and the Burrards cheered the 3–2 victory.

The field cleared very quickly as girls rushed to waiting cars. Alecia collapsed heavily onto the bench and let out a long, exhausted sigh. It had been a tough battle. Still, she felt she had played well, kept up her share of the work. She couldn't wait for a hot bath and lunch.

Suddenly she noticed two white flakes on the bench beside her, then another couple on her bag, and more on the sleeve of her coat. She grinned.

"It's snowing!" she cried. Huge, fat flakes fell from the sky, sticking to the frozen ground and everything else they touched.

"Great," a voice muttered from behind Alecia, "now I'll have to shovel the driveway." Alecia turned to see her friend, Connor Stevens, standing there, gazing up at the sky with a forlorn look on his face. "I swear it does this just to annoy me."

"Dude, you are so pathetic," Alecia said, shaking her head. "I'll help you shovel the driveway, when there's enough snow to shovel!"

"Yes," added Laurie, joining them. "And knowing you, Connor, you'll let your friends do all the work while you 'supervise' from the living room!"

"Hey, you guys, leave poor Connor alone. He lives a hard life," Jeremy told them, passing by with the mesh bag of practice balls. "You coming home, Leesh?" he asked.

Alecia looked up at her stepfather and nodded. "Darn right I am. I'm freezing. I'll see you guys tonight, right?" she asked, looking back at Laurie and Connor.

"Definitely. What time are we meeting at the theatre?" Laurie asked.

"I think the show starts at seven-thirty, so we should be there by seven at the latest," Alecia told them. "Is Annie coming?"

"No," Connor said, shaking his head. "She has a family thing tonight that she couldn't get out of, so it's just the three of us. Unless you wanted to invite Monica along."

Alecia stuck her tongue out at Connor. "As a matter of fact, you could go ahead and invite Monica if you like, but she won't come. I happen to know she's got something else going on. She told me so in band class yesterday. Of course it took her half an hour to tell me," she said, then reddened as Connor shot her a dirty look. "Sorry. You have to admit, though, I'm much better than I was."

"Yeah, okay. I'll give you that. You're better than you were," Connor agreed. "Not that there still isn't plenty of room for improvement."

Alecia casually began swatting Connor with her hand. In another second Laurie was in on the action too, and poor Connor could only defend himself feebly as the girls hit him.

"Enough already!" he cried from beneath their fast-moving arms.

"Take it back!" Alecia demanded, landing a particularly good hit on his head. "I'm perfect. Tell me I'm perfect."

"No way!" Connor cried. "That would be heresy!

I'd be burned at the stake!"

"That's enough, girls," Jeremy said. "Leave the poor boy alone."

"He asked for it."

"Granted," Jeremy allowed, nodding, "the boy can be irritating and annoying. But he has had his punishment. And besides," he said, pausing to look around him, "it's cold out here, I'm hungry, and I'd like to watch the snow fall from inside the house."

"Yeah," Laurie agreed. She had zipped up her bag and was waiting impatiently. "I'm hungry, Connor. Take me home," she demanded.

Connor took Laurie's hand and headed off the field. "See you later!" he called back.

Alecia stuffed her sweat-soaked shin pads, water bottle, and cleats into her bag then headed for the parking lot. Jeremy had the car running and it was nice and warm by the time Alecia crawled in. She leaned back in her seat and closed her eyes. It had been a hard-fought win today.

"Good game today, Leesh," Jeremy told her, patting her thigh. She opened her eyes and grinned at him.

"Thanks."

"I'm really pleased with the way you girls have become a team. You work together very well, reading each other, reading the play. You have a good chance of going all the way this season. We just have to keep it going."

Alecia felt a warm glow spread through her. "We have a good coach," she told him, throwing back the compliment. Jeremy smiled at her.

"Hey, guess what," he said after a while, looking over at Alecia. "I got a call the other day from a guy I worked with years ago. Apparently he heard I'm coaching the Burrards and he asked if there was any room on the team for a good player."

"What'd you tell him?" Alecia asked, putting a hand over her grumbling stomach. She was starving.

"I told him we're always looking for a good player and with Annie off the team, we have that hole in forward to fill. It's not been a huge problem, but it would be nice to have the numbers up. Her name is Alexandra Thomas. She's eager to play again. He's bringing her out on Tuesday. I think she'll be going to your school as well, in grade eight."

"Why didn't she come out today and help in the game if she is so wonderful?" Alecia said, scowling all of a sudden.

"What's with the attitude?" Jeremy asked.

"I don't have an attitude. I just don't know why you're getting so excited about some new girl. Is she a really awesome player or something?" Alecia felt Jeremy's stare and cleared her throat. She had been working hard at accepting change a little more graciously, but it was hard and she had to struggle now. The team was good the way it was, why wreck things with an unknown player? What if she didn't fit in with the others? What if she wasn't all that good and dragged them down?

"I understand that she is quite good. Give her a chance before you turn against her," Jeremy said, glancing pointedly at Alecia.

"Yeah. Sure. Whatever you say," she muttered, and let the subject drop.

2 OLD PHOTOS

By the time Alecia had eaten the homemade seafood chowder and grilled cheese sandwiches her mother had prepared, and soaked in a very hot bath for a long time, the few flurries had turned into a near whiteout. Alecia grinned as she pressed her nose against the window, watching eagerly as the world outside gradually disappeared beneath a blanket of feathery white flakes.

"It sure is covering fast," her mother said, coming to stand beside her. She put an arm around Alecia's waist and hugged her tightly. "I hope the roads will be okay."

"They won't be, but we don't have to go anywhere, so we're all right," Jeremy said from his chair by the fire. Alecia glanced at him and grinned. He wouldn't move for the rest of the weekend if he could help it.

"What about our movie tonight?" Alecia asked, suddenly remembering. Her grin slid a little. She did not like having to cancel plans.

Jeremy looked up from his book and eyed her silently for several seconds. "Can't control the weather,

Leesh," he said at last. "But why don't we wait a few hours and see what happens? It's barely one o'clock." Grudgingly, Alecia allowed there was lots of time before seven. She turned back to the quickly whitening view outside the window.

"So, did you play well today?" her mother asked. Mrs. Parker was a fair-weather fan. On days like this she preferred to lend her support mentally rather than physically. Alecia didn't mind. She felt the same way about cold days. She would have preferred to stay home where it was warm too. Still, she loved playing soccer. And she really liked that she played on such a strong team. They hadn't always been so strong. Last season, with Mike as their coach, they had sat in the bottom half of their league all season, winning barely half of their games. This year they were eight and two. They missed Anne, who had quit in November, but Laurie was a great captain and they were on top of their game.

"I played pretty well. No goals, actually," Alecia said, thinking about it. "I didn't even get an assist, but I was pretty strong. They pushed us hard today. Before Christmas they weren't much of a threat. But today!" She shook her head. "We don't play them again for a while."

"That's my girl. By the way," Mrs. Parker said, moving away from Alecia. She went over to the dining room table and rummaged around in the pile of papers stacked there. "I found these when I was cleaning out a drawer this morning. I thought you might like to look at them." She handed a stack of photographs to Alecia, who had joined her at the table. "They are of your father and you and me."

Alecia looked up at her mother, her eyes wide, then she moved to the sofa and began looking through the pictures. Her father had died when Alecia was four. She didn't remember him at all, although her mother spoke of him all the time and they had some pictures around the house. Not as many since her mother and Jeremy had married the previous July, but there was a nice one of the three of them that sat on Alecia's bedside table and another that hung in the hall upstairs. But these she had never seen before.

"Why have I never seen these?" she asked, smiling at the faces and silly poses. There were her parents dressed up for Halloween as Tweedledee and Tweedledum from *Alice in Wonderland*.

"They got stuck in with some paperwork. I only found them today because I needed an old form. That's you and Dad on your third birthday. You had insisted on wearing that ridiculous dress that was way too small. You screamed so loud Peter finally just put it on you. Of course it was too tight, so then you screamed to get it off. I barely had a chance to take the picture."

Alecia touched the face of her three-year-old self gently. She often wished that she had known her dad. Even just to have one memory that was hers, and not stolen from a picture or from her mother's stories. She picked up another shot.

"That's out at Grandma Ellie's cottage on Okanagan Lake," Alecia said, frowning at the picture of her and her parents in a rowboat. Behind them spread the wide blueness of the lake.

"That's right. You had just turned four. That was the summer before Peter got sick," Mrs. Parker said softly. She cleared her throat quickly and then laughed, remembering. "Grandma Ellie fell in the lake after she took that picture. I don't know how she managed to do it, either. She handed the camera to Grandpa Don, telling him to make sure he put it someplace safe, not like last time, and then she took a step and was in the lake. We laughed so hard we almost capsized the boat!"

From his chair Jeremy joined in the laughter and Alecia suddenly remembered that he was there. Then she felt guilty. Here they were remembering their old life, leaving Jeremy out completely. She looked over and caught his eye. He was watching them carefully, but didn't seem sad, or left out. In fact, Alecia thought he looked thoughtful.

"Did you want to see these?" she asked, holding them out. Jeremy shook his head.

"I'll look at them later, sweetie. You enjoy them." Alecia flipped through the pile of photos, smiling at some, uninterested in others, until she found a photograph that made her stop. It was a black–and–white photo of her father taken at his university graduation. Alecia knew her father had graduated from Simon Fraser University. It was where her parents had met twenty years ago. She picked the print up, glancing quickly at her mother. He looked so young, staring at her with serious eyes. He seemed to be speaking to her, trying to tell her something. She glanced at her mother again, then slipped the photo onto her lap.

★ ★ ★

Sunday Alecia woke up to a white world. She knelt on her bed and leaned her elbows on the window-sill, grinning out at the altered landscape that was their backyard.

Everything looked different, unfamiliar. Her favourite tree, a red maple that offered wonderful cool shade in the summer, looked like a bony old skeleton doing some kind of macabre dance. In the lane some of the neighbourhood children were already constructing a snowman, their voices reaching Alecia over the stillness.

They had managed to get out to the movies last night, barely. It had been a bit of a fight with Jeremy to get him to drive her to the theatres, but in the end he had agreed. It wasn't far and the roads were all flat. Plus the snowplows had cleared most of the main roads. Alecia was glad they had gone. She hated cancelling plans, hated things to not happen when she had been looking forward to them.

"Leesh? You up?" a voice called from the hall and Alecia pulled her attention from the window. She crawled off the bed and went to the door. Her mother was standing at the bottom of the stairs, dressed to go out.

"What's up?" Alecia asked, yawning.

"Jeremy and I are going for a walk. We'll be back in an hour or so."

"It's cold out there," Alecia reminded her, cheekily. Her mother stuck out her tongue.

"I've got my sweetie to keep me warm," Mrs. Parker told her.

"Have fun," Alecia said, turning back to her room.

She had a quick shower, dressed, and tidied her room, then wandered downstairs. She found herself some breakfast and took it to the living room to eat in front of the TV. Feet braced against the coffee table she slurped cereal into her mouth, staring blankly at the cartoons she found. She had a ton of homework to do, she remembered, and a test in French on Tuesday. Plus, she hadn't practised her clarinet in days.

But Alecia wasn't quite ready to tackle those things just yet. Instead she leaned forward to put her bowl on the table. Sitting where she had left them yesterday were the photographs her mother had shown her. She picked them up and began flipping through them again.

She had hidden the grad photo in her room, wanting, for some reason, to keep it for herself. She knew her mother wouldn't mind, but still, she didn't want her to know. Who had her father been? Had he been nice? Quick tempered? Had he resisted change as much as Alecia did? Maybe he had been adventurous and eager for new things. Alecia hated anything new.

An ad came on the TV, breaking into her thoughts. The woman was so excited about her product that Alecia found herself listening despite herself. The woman held a kit for making scrapbooks called a Memory Maker. She positively buzzed with the thrill of it.

"Only $49.95 plus shipping and handling!" she cried. "What a great deal! Get yours while they last! Operators are standing by!"

Alecia sat forward, a plan forming in her head as the woman showed all the miracles of her product.

Could she do one of those? About her dad? Construct herself some memories of her father? Alecia wondered. She picked up a couple of the photos lying in her lap and stared at them. Why not? What would be wrong with that? she wondered.

Forgetting all about the homework waiting for her, Alecia went off in search of a photo album. Her mother kept a supply on hand to put photos in as soon as they arrived in the house. It was utterly amazing that the little pile she had found yesterday had not been put in one already. Alecia found a nice manly looking one she liked and took it to her room.

On the inside cover, using pencil, she wrote:

The Life And Times Of Peter Sheffield: My Father

Then she went over the letters carefully in black felt pen. She smiled, happy with the effect, then stopped, frowning. Now what? she wondered. She didn't have anything to put in an album — her father had been dead for nine years. What was she thinking? Silly fool. All she had were some old photos her mother had given her. There were no little mementos from outings, no pieces of clothing, nothing.

Alecia lay flat on the bed, holding the scrapbook in her arms. Well, she would just have to start hunting. Surely there were things around the house, stored away safely. Her mother never threw anything away. She still had all of Alecia's baby clothes and most of her toys. She claimed they were for when Alecia had children of her own one day but Alecia was pretty sure it was more because her mother couldn't bear to part with things. There must be stuff of her father's.

And maybe Alecia could casually call her grandparents. Grandma Ellie was just as bad as Mom — you'd think they were mother and daughter. She would have kept something of her son's. Alecia was pretty sure that if she asked, her grandmother would let her have something. She began to feel a bit better and sat up. She just needed to be patient, that was all. She couldn't expect everything to fall into place just like that. It would take planning and a little detective work.

3 "IT'S *LEXI*"

"And you wouldn't believe how much I ate! I was such a pig. But you know how Chinese food is, you can eat and eat. Everything is so good and there is so much of it! Plus it was a buffet, which is even worse," Monica said and then paused to wave to someone. She flipped her long, brown hair over her shoulder and frowned slightly at Anne and Alecia.

"What was I saying?" she asked. "Oh, right, dinner. There was this guy at our table, I don't know, someone's third cousin once removed or whatever, and he was so cute. I mean, I could hardly talk all night from looking at him. He was too far away for me to really say anything to him, but I did smile lots and stuff, you know. You have to flirt a little, right? Isn't that a girl's prerogative or something?"

"I thought it was to change your mind," Alecia said, since Monica had stopped to catch her breath.

"A girl's prerogative is to change her mind?" Monica repeated, thinking about it. "I don't know if I've ever heard that before."

27

"I've heard it," Anne said, coming out of her thoughts to join the conversation. "My mother says it all the time to Dad. He figures she uses it on a 'needs be' basis. They're always talking like that. Half the time I can't understand a word they say," she finished, laughing.

Alecia moved her clarinet case to her left hand and winced slightly. A check she'd taken during the game on Saturday had bruised her right shoulder and it was still sore today. She wondered if it was a good enough excuse to get out of gym class that day. Alecia pulled open the door to the school and the three friends went inside.

"Did I tell you about Jeremy's news?" Alecia asked as she and Anne headed for their lockers. "A new girl is starting on the team. Her name is Alexandra Thomas. She's supposed to be pretty good."

"Really? That would help, wouldn't it?" Anne asked.

"I guess. I think we're doing okay by ourselves, though."

"Well, it never hurts to have extra players. You know, in case someone gets hurt or something." Anne was always optimistic, always accepting of anything new. She never saw anything as negative. Sometimes it drove Alecia nuts.

"You could come back," she said. Anne smiled and shook her head.

"Not until September, Leesh," she reminded her. Alecia scowled and shoved her clarinet into her locker. She didn't think they needed any new players. But no one else seemed to agree with her.

★ ★ ★

Alexandra Thomas had already arrived and was waiting outside when Jeremy and Alecia got to the school Tuesday night. She was dressed in ratty jeans and an old jersey and was leaning against the gym door, her arms folded across her chest. Alecia stole a quick glance at the girl as she helped Jeremy unload the car. Her hair, cut short to her chin, was dark and straight. She was taller than Alecia, but not by much, and heavier. She watched as Jeremy and Alecia unloaded the mesh bag of balls and the stack of orange cones and carried them to the door. She didn't offer to help.

Alecia cleared her throat, determined to start off being friendly and welcoming. "Hi. You must be Alexandra," she said with a smile. "I'm Alecia, and that's Jeremy, our coach, over there."

"It's *Lexi*," the girl said. Alecia glanced at her, but said nothing as they got the equipment inside. In another minute the others arrived and there wasn't another chance to say anything to *Lexi*.

No one had known a new girl was starting that night, and they eyed her curiously while waiting for Jeremy to begin practice. Lexi stood near the stage, her arms still crossed, a slight frown on her face. When Jeremy called them all together, she came and stood behind them.

"We have a new player tonight," Jeremy said. "This is Alexandra Thomas, and she'll be playing forward for us. Welcome to the Burrards, Alexandra." He smiled at her and a couple of the girls turned and said hi. Lexi ignored them. She glared at Jeremy.

"It's *Lexi*," she said in the same tone she'd used on Alecia. Alecia glanced at Jeremy and caught his smile slip ever so slightly.

"All right, Lexi. Let's start off with three laps around the gym. And no cutting corners this time."

Jeremy told the girls to pair off after their warm-up and they spread out around the gym to practise dribbling. Everyone quickly found a partner, leaving Lexi standing by herself. Alecia felt slightly guilty, but ignored it. It wasn't her responsibility to babysit the new girl. Let Laurie do it; she was captain. She turned her attention to her own partner, Rianne, and the drill they had been told to work on.

In another second Laurie had grabbed Lexi by the arm and pulled her off to work with her and Nancy. Rianne stopped the ball with her foot and watched as the other girls worked their drill. A small frown formed on her forehead. "You know, I think I recognize her," she said when Alecia came up beside her. "I think she used to play with my cousin."

"Oh yeah? Is she any good?" Alecia asked.

"She thought so," Rianne said. She watched Lexi for another second then turned back to Alecia and shrugged. Alecia glanced at Lexi again, curious. Was she any good or had they just added dead wood to their team? she wondered.

They worked on their drill for a while, then Jeremy divided them into two groups and they worked at each end of the gym with the goalkeepers, Stacie and Karen. Alecia found herself on Lexi's team with Laurie and Stacie and a few other girls. They lined up and Laurie started them off by kicking a shot at Stacie. Stacie blocked it easily and sent it back to the next girl in line. Finally Alecia took her turn, kicking high over Stacie's right shoulder. She almost cheered, knowing it was a good shot, then she watched in amazement as Stacie dove backwards and caught the ball, grinning cheekily at Alecia as she sent it back out.

Lexi raised her eyebrows, frowning slightly. "Pretty confident, isn't she?" she asked.

"Yes, and we like her that way," Laurie replied politely.

Lexi didn't say anything as she moved forward in the line. She caught the ball as Stacie passed it to her. Carefully she set herself up, taking her time before kicking the ball at the net. It came at Stacie on an angle, heading toward the far post of the goal. Stacie lunged for it, but missed and the ball rolled past her. Lexi looked around smugly at the other girls.

"Nice shot, Lexi," Laurie said, but the other girls just turned away.

★ ★ ★

Practice finished at seven-thirty and the girls quickly disappeared as parents arrived to drive them home. Alecia and Jeremy loaded the car and Alecia scrambled in while Jeremy checked the gym one last time.

"All set?" he asked as he climbed in behind the wheel a second later.

"Hey," Alecia said, not answering his question, "who is that?" She pointed to the school where a dark shape could just be seen walking along the building.

Jeremy frowned then climbed out of the car again. "Excuse me?" he called. "Did you need a ride somewhere?"

The figure turned and in the light coming from a classroom, Alecia realized it was the new girl. It was a cold January night and there was still snow on the ground from the storm over the weekend, but Lexi was wearing only the jersey they had seen her in earlier.

"No. I'm fine," she called, her voice as cool as the night air.

"I don't like my players walking home alone," Jeremy told her. "Especially dressed the way you are. Did someone forget to come get you?"

"No, I'm fine, I told you."

"Hold on a sec, Leesh," Jeremy said, then closed the car door and walked toward the girl. Alecia watched as he approached Lexi. She couldn't hear what they were saying, but she could hear Lexi's voice in her head, slightly scornful, slightly rude. She hadn't exactly made a good first impression on the Burrards. It was quite a change from Anne's sunny smile and cheerful optimism, that was for sure.

Jeremy came back alone and climbed into the car without saying a word. Lexi had disappeared. "That is one interesting girl," he said, shaking his head. "She insisted that she was fine. That her ride would be along any second and to just leave her alone. I tried telling her that as her coach I was responsible for her until someone showed up. I could see she was going to keep arguing with me but then she turned, waved at a car coming along the street and dashed off." Jeremy shrugged as he turned on the ignition. "Takes all kinds I guess."

"Aren't you friends with her dad?" Alecia asked as Jeremy drove up their driveway and into the garage. They pulled the gear out of the trunk and tossed it in the corner, then made their way into the house.

"We were never friends," Jeremy said. "More acquaintances than anything. I certainly don't know anything about his family or home life."

"Oh well, maybe they're one of those families that insists on lots of independence," Alecia said slyly. "You know, give the teenager lots of space and let her do what she wants."

"Yeah, maybe. Not like around here, huh?" Jeremy tossed back, grinning at her.

4 NEW IDEAS

After school on Wednesday Alecia found Anne and Connor waiting beneath one of the leafless oaks in the schoolyard. She looked in surprise at Connor. He almost always walked home from school with Laurie, who lived in the opposite direction to Alecia and her friends.

"Where's Laurie today?" she asked.

"Getting some extra help with some work," Connor told her.

"So we get honoured with your presence then, do we?" she asked, dodging the hand that whipped out to hit her. She dropped her bag on the grass and sighed heavily. "I am so beat!" she cried. "That quiz in English nearly killed me."

"Helps if you study," Connor reminded her. Alecia ignored him as she looked through her bag. As she stood up again she spotted Lexi coming through the doors. She buried her head in her pack, hoping the other girl wouldn't notice her.

"Hi Alecia," Lexi said, noticing Alecia and her friends, despite Alecia's attempt to hide. She approached slowly, hesitantly.

"Oh, hi Lexi," Alecia said coolly, glancing at the other girl. "How are things going?"

"Not bad. I only got lost once today."

"Happens to everyone," Connor told her, laughing.

"Are you the Lexi who joined the Burrards?" Anne asked, introducing herself since Alecia obviously wasn't going to. "I'm Anne. And this is Connor."

"Nice to meet you," Lexi said, smiling shyly at Anne and Connor. She glanced once more at Alecia, who was very busy studying the toe of her shoe.

"Well, I guess I should get going home," she said finally. "See you around."

"Yeah, see you later, Lexi," Alecia called after her retreating back.

"She seems okay, Leesh," Anne commented as they headed out of the school grounds.

Alecia shrugged. "She's kind of full of herself. She scored on Stacie last night and positively gloated about it the rest of the night."

"Maybe she was just nervous, her first night," Anne suggested, ever the peacemaker. Alecia shrugged again and Anne dropped the subject.

"This is kind of nice," Anne said after a while. "Just the three of us. Not that I don't like Laurie or Monica," she said quickly, anxious not to be misunderstood.

"We know how much you hate Laurie," Connor said.

"I don't —" Anne began, then caught sight of Connor's grin and stopped. "She's really such a pain, Connor. I don't know what you see in her."

"I know what you mean," Alecia broke in, "about just the three of us. Everything is so different now than it was in September."

"Yeah, but different in good ways, I think," Connor said. "Things can't stay the same forever."

Alecia would have argued that life would be much simpler if they did stay the same. For years it had just been the three of them — Alecia, Anne, and Connor. Now there were boyfriends and girlfriends, new players on the team, and a Valentine's dance that Monica was all excited about.

But it wasn't just new people and things, Alecia realized. The three friends themselves were all changing so much as well. Annie was more outspoken and confident; Connor was taller and his voice had deepened. And Alecia, too, had changed. She had grown and her clothes didn't fit the same anymore.

"You off, Annie?" Connor asked as they paused at the end of Anne's driveway.

"Yeah. I'll see you both tomorrow," she said and gave a little wave as she headed for the house.

"You're awfully quiet today, Leesh," Connor said after a while. "Something wrong?"

"No, not really, I guess. Monica kind of annoyed me at lunch today. The way she was going on and on about that dance. Really, she can be so dense sometimes."

"You don't have to go if you don't want to," Connor reminded her.

"Really? Really I don't? You mean Monica's word isn't law? We don't have to all bow down to her loud opinion?"

"Take it easy, Leesh. You know that's just the way Monica is. It's just her way."

"Well, she should change, then," Alecia snapped. Why was she so upset? she wondered. She took a deep breath and let it out slowly. "It just annoys me that she assumes everyone will be as thrilled as she is about stuff. I don't like dances and things like that."

Connor adjusted his backpack on his shoulder and walked silently for a while. "You know, sometimes I think you just get mad at things because you don't want to deal with them. I think maybe you do want to go to the dance, but you're scared to. Maybe you'll have a good time."

"Oh, spare me! Don't start with your 'Dr. Stevens, psychiatrist' routine! I get so tired of having everything I say and do analyzed by you. Do you do that to Laurie, too? Because I'm surprised she sticks around if you do."

"Blah, blah, blah. You need me to analyze your be-haviour, otherwise you'd never know anything," he said, pausing to scoop a handful of old snow from the pile by the curb. He tossed it at Alecia, but it missed and landed with a soft plop on the ground. "It might be fun, you know. Maybe if all of us went as a group it would be okay."

Alecia was quiet and Connor said nothing more about it. At Alecia's driveway he stopped for a second. They looked at each other, Alecia still scowling, Connor serious. Then suddenly Alecia started to laugh. "I'll think about it, okay?" she said.

"That's all I ask," he said, his face solemn, though his eyes twinkled.

"Wanna come in for a while? It's been ages since you've been over," Alecia asked.

"I could for a while, I guess. I'm in no hurry to get to my homework. I'm jealous of your empty house, Leesh," Connor said, kicking off his shoes at the front door. He dropped his pack and coat on top of them and followed Alecia through to the kitchen.

"Your house is empty a lot too," she reminded him. "Now that Gillian is working part-time."

"Ah, but she still comes back. That's the problem with sisters."

"Did you want something to drink or eat?"

"You mean there is actually something to eat in this place? When was the last time someone found time to shop?" Connor asked, sliding into a chair at the table.

"How about a bagel with cream cheese? Will that do?" Alecia offered, ignoring the comment. It was no secret that shopping was done as a last resort around the Parker house.

They finished eating and wandered upstairs to Alecia's room. Connor grabbed Alecia's iPod off her desk and began scrolling through her playlist.

"What you got to listen to anyway?" he asked. He fussed for a long time before finally settling on something. He pressed play and went to sit on the bed.

"Hey, is this a new photo?" he asked. Alecia came and looked over his shoulder. The photo was of her father, taken the Christmas before he died.

"Yeah," Alecia said softly.

"He was pretty good-looking," Connor said and Alecia felt a little glow of pleasure at the words. No one she knew now had known her father, except her mother, and Alecia expected her to think him handsome. She'd married him after all.

"He was, yes. My mother says he was one of the handsomest guys she knew."

"So what happened to you?" he said, turning away. He flopped down on the bed again and tucked his hands behind his head.

"Do you think about him a lot, Leesh?" he asked a second later, rolling over to look at her.

When didn't she think about him? she wondered. She thought of the scrapbook lying safely under the mattress. Since Sunday she had discovered two more photos in the pile from downstairs.

"Sometimes, I guess," she lied, fidgeting with her stuffed animals.

"I'd have so many questions," Connor went on, returning the frame to its place on the bedside table. "I would be driving my mother nuts with them. I have questions about my dad and I live with him every day. I've always wanted to know, for example, why he is so athletic and I'm so pathetic at sports."

"I have some questions," Alecia admitted. "Maybe I'll ask someday."

"Maybe Jeremy will adopt you. Do you think he would?" Connor asked suddenly. He sat up, leaning forward eagerly. "That would be awesome, eh? You'd have his last name and you'd have a dad again. Jeremy would have a daughter."

"Why would he want to do that? Things are fine the way they are. We get along great. Besides, I have a name. I have my dad's name." The idea upset her, made her stomach do strange things.

"I know, but you don't have him. You never even knew him."

"It doesn't seem fair to my dad to let someone else take his place. It sounds disrespectful or something. Besides, no one is talking about adopting anyone. Let's go watch TV," she said and bounced out of the room before Connor could say anything further.

★ ★ ★

Connor left an hour later and Alecia was kind of glad to see him go. His words had not left her, had stayed in a corner of her mind, poking at her while they watched old reruns on TV. She felt strangely unsettled, close to tears. She had never thought about Jeremy in that way before. Never thought about her name. Things were good the way they were, weren't they? She had no problem with any of it. She didn't want to change her name. Change her identity. She was Alecia Sheffield. Wouldn't she be a different person if her name changed to Parker? But then, she told herself sternly, no one was asking her to change it.

Jeremy had never once mentioned the idea of adopting her. He knew things were fine the way they were. He liked being her stepfather. Liked the relationship the way it was. Why would a forty-year-old man want to suddenly adopt a silly teenaged girl? Alecia laughed out loud, telling herself to stop being ridiculous. Connor had put silly thoughts in her head and she just needed to forget about them. She went to the stereo and popped a CD into the player, turning the volume up as loud as she could stand it.

"Whoa!" Jeremy cried, coming in from the garage ten minutes later. "What is with the brain-numbing noise?"

"WHAT?" Alecia cried, holding a hand to her

ear. "I CAN'T HEAR YOU! THE MUSIC IS TOO LOUD!"

"Then turn it down," her mother said, lowering the volume. "You'll wreck your eardrums listening to it that loud," she said, frowning. "You know better than that."

"It's a teenage thing," Jeremy told her seriously. He grabbed Alecia's hands and they danced around the living room to the thumping beat from the stereo. "You were never a teenager, so you wouldn't understand."

"I was a teenager, for your information. And I could dance with the best of them. In fact, I nearly won a contest in grade eleven. So there," Mrs. Parker said, shaking her head as she watched Alecia and Jeremy swing around the room bumping into furniture and against the walls.

"Don't listen to her, Leesh," Jeremy said in a mock whisper. "She's just trying to save face. She told me once that she thought dancing was evil. And rock music even worse. I think it was her upbringing."

"Jeremy Parker! Stop filling my daughter's head with nonsense."

Alecia was laughing so hard she thought she was going to throw up as Jeremy whirled her around and around the room, dipping her almost to the floor, swinging her under his arm, pulling her back in. Then suddenly the music changed, becoming slow and soft. Jeremy put an arm around her waist, took her hand with his and pulled her close.

"Ah, this is even better. I always liked these dances best. Sweaty palms not withstanding. Put your feet on top of mine, Leesh, and I'll guide you along. Your mother just doesn't understand the pleasures of a good dance."

"I think I'll make some dinner," Mrs. Parker said and left the room.

"I hear there's a dance at school next month," Jeremy said, moving them easily. He was a wonderful dancer, Alecia realized, not that she knew a lot about it. But he certainly seemed confident and easy, moving gracefully in time with the music.

"How did you hear that? I only found out about it today," Alecia said, pulling back to look up at him. Jeremy grinned at her.

"I have my ways," was all he said. "I guess you and your tribe will be going?"

"Monica certainly wants to, and probably Connor will take Laurie. But Annie and I aren't interested. Who would we dance with? And besides, dances are silly."

Jeremy stopped moving abruptly, nearly sending Alecia to the floor. "This is silly? I thought we were having fun," he said, sounding hurt. Alecia felt a little guilty and tried to back up.

"Not this. This is fun. But you're different than a room full of silly boys who shove each other and say stupid things and get all goofy and idiotic. You know how to dance."

"Ahh. Now I see. Well, I can't do much about the school full of goofy boys. But it might be fun anyway. You could dance with Anne or Connor. Right? I think you should give it a try." He started dancing again, humming softly to the music.

"Well, I don't want to go. So drop it, okay?" Alecia told him, annoyed. He had ruined a perfectly good time with his nonsense.

"Consider the matter dropped, my dear. I believe your mother is preparing dinner for us. Shall we help her out?" Jeremy asked, dropping her hand to bow before her. He was the most ridiculous person sometimes, Alecia thought as she followed him into the kitchen. The most ridiculous person on earth. But she smiled anyway.

5 TEAMWORK?!

A sudden warm spell and two days of steady rain had washed most of the remaining snow away and by Sunday morning the field was a sodden mess, but clear enough to play. The team the Burrards were up against, the Whitecaps, were unknown to Alecia and her teammates. They had played only one game against them the year before and none so far this season. Jeremy believed strongly in knowing your opponent and they spent a lot of time analyzing the other teams in the league, but these girls had been hard to analyze.

They were gathered around the bench Sunday morning, stretching and loosening up, eyeing the other girls as they came onto the field to warm up. They seemed to be about the same size as the Burrards, and Rianne recognized one of the defence. "She goes to our church. She doesn't look very big."

"Yeah, but is she any good?" Nancy asked. Rianne shrugged.

"What about her?" Stacie asked, pointing to a tall

girl wearing a purple jacket over her uniform. "She looks like some of the Rocketeer forwards."

"She looks kind of spacey to me. She probably spends most of the time on the bench," Rianne said.

"Well, at least they probably know all their players. Not like us," Stacie grumbled. "I think it's ridiculous bringing in a new player at this point in the season. I mean, how are we supposed to play like a team when we don't know everyone?"

"Stacie, you've got to give people a chance. Maybe if we tried to get to know Lexi instead of just calling her down, she'd warm up to us. After all, she doesn't know us either," Laurie said. Her voice was low and gentle and Stacie flushed a little, muttering an apology. "Really, guys. We just need to talk to her, get to know her a little. It works."

As if to help Laurie prove her point, Lexi chose that moment to show up. She tossed her bag on the bench, glancing briefly around at the other girls as she sat down beside it.

"Hi, Lexi," Laurie said, giving the girl a friendly smile. "We were just trying to get a reading on the other team. We haven't played them before. Have you ever heard anything about them?"

"What would I have heard?" Lexi asked.

"I don't know, I just wondered if you had, that's all. We always try and have a bit of knowledge about the team we're playing against. You know, who their good strikers are, how they use their defence, that kind of thing."

"I don't know anything about them. On my old team we worried about ourselves, not everyone else," Lexi said, turning to her bag. She pulled out her cleats and dropped them to the ground. Laurie and Alecia exchanged glances but said nothing. Eventually the girls drifted away, leaving Lexi alone on the bench.

"We don't know this team," Jeremy said in his pre-game talk. "But that doesn't mean we can't beat them. This morning I want you to pay close attention to where everyone else is on the field. That means you have to keep your head up at all times and talk to each other, encourage each other. It's cold today and I plan to rotate players a lot, so be aware of people coming off and going on. Look to Laurie for leadership. Protect our goalkeeper. Stacie, smother the ball whenever you can — I've heard these guys are pretty good with the rebounds. Let's not give them any, okay? Right, let's play."

Alecia took up her position as midfielder behind and to the left of Lexi. On the other side were Allison and Marnie. Laurie got the opening kick and sent it across to Allison, who sent it right back to Laurie. Very quickly they moved in to the Whitecaps' end with a series of tight little passes. Laurie, about to be tackled by a charging forward, passed the ball to Lexi, who caught it and moved toward the net. She took a quick shot on goal, but the goalkeeper blocked it and kicked it back out into play. The Whitecaps' centre caught the kick and ran back toward the Burrards' end, but Lexi was on her in seconds and stole it away. She turned quickly and headed back for the net. This time she held the ball, adeptly keeping it from the opposing midfielder who kept challenging her. The other Burrards hurried to get in position.

"Where is everyone?" Lexi screamed as she juggled the ball, waiting for someone to pass to. There were Whitecaps players all over her and, although the rest of the Burrards were doing their best, there was no clear shot. Finally the ball rolled out of bounds.

"Keep with the play, you guys!" Lexi called. "Keep your eyes on the ball. I could have scored there if there had been someone to help me set up the play."

Most of the girls ignored her. Who was she to tell them what to do, how to play? That was Jeremy's and Laurie's job. The ball was thrown into play and was quickly picked off by the Whitecaps' centre. She kicked it ahead of her to a waiting forward, but the pass was intercepted by Lexi, who practically sent the forward to the ground as she tackled her for possession of the ball. There was no whistle, despite the dirty looks from the Whitecaps players who saw her. Play continued down the field with Lexi carrying the ball almost the whole way herself. Her second shot on net was closer than the first, but still missed and rolled out of bounds.

"Nice try, Lexi," Laurie called as they passed each other on the field. "Next time it'll get in."

"Yeah, thanks," Lexi answered, wiping her hands on her shorts. She was already a mess — her hair wild around her face, her eyes large and dark. Alecia looked down at her own clean uniform. Lexi really threw herself into the game, that was for sure. She was like Stacie — unconcerned about getting dirty, intent only on winning. Still, her habit of telling the others how to play was already getting annoying. Twice she had made comments to Alecia, which Alecia had ignored. Everyone was relieved when Jeremy sent Rianne in for her and Lexi left the field.

Lexi off the field was hardly better than Lexi on the field, however. Her voice could be heard above everyone else's, even Jeremy's.

"Get in low, Rianne, you're not low enough!"

"Where are your hands, Stacie! Keep them up, keep them out front!"

"That was a pretty weak pass, Allison. You gotta give it more than that," she called, pacing up and down the field. She didn't stop shouting until Jeremy told her to. Then, if anyone got close enough to the side of the field where she was standing, they could hear her muttering under her breath so Jeremy couldn't hear.

Allison managed to score, finally, just before the end of the first half and they left the field ahead by one.

"That was great, Allison," Laurie said, patting the girl on the back as they left the field together. One by one the other players congratulated Allison on her unassisted goal. It hadn't been pretty — she had intercepted a pass from the other team and kicked wildly at the net — but it had gone in. And heading into the second half with the lead was a good thing.

"It wasn't very nice looking, but what the heck! They can't all be beauties," Allison said, pleased with herself despite her words. The others laughed.

"Good job. It always helps to get the first goal," Lexi said. "But you might want to try giving yourself a second to set up before you shoot. And get centred over your midline. It helps to direct the ball. There was plenty of time to set it up well." Allison looked as though she wasn't quite sure how to respond. She was saved from having to say anything by Laurie, who stepped in, smiling at Lexi. "I'm sure those are good ideas, but we usually analyze our play at practice, not during a game. Jeremy likes us to focus on winning."

"By Tuesday everyone will have forgotten what they did wrong today. You have to point it out right away," Lexi argued, standing squarely in front of Laurie.

"Well, maybe on your other team that's the way it was done," Laurie said, keeping her voice even, "but Jeremy likes to discuss the game later."

Teamwork?!

"I would have thought, as captain, you would want to help your players become better, but whatever," Lexi said and walked away, leaving the rest of the Burrards staring after her in stunned silence.

6 TROUBLE WITH LEXI

On Wednesday afternoon Alecia left the school with Monica and Anne, but just on the other side of the fence she stopped walking.

"I have some things to pick up for Mom at the drugstore. I'll catch you guys tomorrow," she said. Her friends looked at her in surprise.

"Did you want us to come with you?" Anne asked, already changing direction. Alecia quickly stopped her.

"No! No thanks, that's okay. It's out of your way and I can manage," she said. "Really."

"Well," Monica said, shrugging, "see you tomorrow then. Come on, Annie."

Alecia watched them walk away and then turned and headed in the opposite direction. She had heard, in a discussion in one of her classes, that sometimes smells can bring back memories. Alecia knew her father had worn after-shave and the idea had come to her that maybe if she had a bottle, it would help with digging up old memories.

Half an hour later, safely closeted in her room, she pulled the scrapbook from under the mattress where she kept it hidden. No memories came to her when she sniffed at the open bottle, but, she reminded herself, she should give it a chance. Very carefully she took a cotton ball and wiped at the pages of the scrapbook, trying not to get too much on each page. Then she hid the bottle in the farthest corner of her dresser and went back to the bed.

She hadn't attached anything yet. She was waiting until she had everything together before doing that. So far, in two weeks of searching, Alecia had the photos, about six now, a copy of her birth certificate (it had her father's name on it) and, what she was most thrilled about, a handkerchief with her father's initials embroidered in one corner. She had found it one afternoon looking through her mother's dresser for a scarf she wanted to wear. Alecia felt slightly guilty about taking the handkerchief from the drawer, but decided that it was for a good cause and her mother probably didn't know it was in there anyway. It had been hidden way in the back, in the corner.

Still, the little pile seemed rather pathetic as Alecia looked it over now. Hardly anything from thirty years of life. She sighed. It was taking a long time, it seemed, but she wasn't ready to give up. She put everything back in the bag and tucked it under the mattress.

On the way home from the drugstore she'd thought

of something else she could do and leaned over the bed to the bedside table. In the drawer was a small journal Anne had given her for Christmas. Alecia had not known what to do with it, until now. She opened it to the first page, picked up her pen, and started writing.

Dear Dad,

This is Alecia writing. But maybe you know that. Maybe you know everything. I don't really know much about where you are. About heaven. Annie might, she goes to church with her mom every week. I don't go to church. Anyway, I thought, maybe, you might like to get to know me a little. It's been a long time since you've seen me, I've changed a lot. I'm growing and I'm in high school now. Did you know I play soccer? I'm a midfielder. That means I help the strikers and the defence. I don't score a lot of goals, Allison is pretty good at that, but I do get assists. We're a pretty good team, too. Except this new girl has joined and I'm not sure she's going to work out. I mean, she's awfully nasty. Everyone on the team is really upset about it. But Jeremy didn't know. You know Jeremy, don't you? He and Mom got married last July. He's great. But he's not my father. You are. And you always will be.

Love, Alecia

★ ★ ★

Alecia was outside the gym Thursday night before practice, hunting for something in the trunk of the car, when a car pulled into a parking space a few feet away. She leaned her head out to see who it was, but quickly tucked it back when she saw it was Lexi. She didn't have anything to say to her, that was for sure. She heard a car door open but didn't hear it close again.

"Will you be able to pick me up?" she heard Lexi ask a second later. She kept her head down, although she had found what she was looking for.

There was a long sigh from inside the car and an impatient tapping. "It isn't very convenient, Alexandra," a male voice said.

"It's just that it's so dark. I don't like walking by myself," Lexi said, her voice not at all the strong, bossy one she used at practice. She was pleading.

"I can't promise anything. You aren't the only one in this family, despite what you might think," the voice told her.

Alecia stifled a cough. Was that Lexi's dad? She was getting uncomfortable, bent over in the trunk, which smelled an awful lot like the mud and sweat from all the dirty soccer gear that lived in there.

"I know I'm not the only one in the family," Lexi said. And then, a second later added, "Mom always picked me up from practice. She didn't like me walking home alone after dark."

"Don't you start pulling that nonsense on me!" the

man cried, his voice rising slightly. "I don't care what your mother did. You live with me and Brenda now and there won't be any of that spoiling your mother was so good at. Now, go on to your practice before you're late. If I can make it, I'll pick you up."

Alecia heard the door slam shut and footsteps on the pavement. When it was silent, Alecia stood up, stretching out her stiff back muscles, closed the trunk of the car, and headed inside the gym.

She joined Laurie, Stacie, and a few other girls at the bench. They were deep in discussion about the Valentine's dance that was coming up. Alecia groaned as she opened her bag. It was becoming one of the few topics of conversation among her friends. Laurie grinned at her and tapped her foot.

"You bought your ticket for the dance yet, Leesh?" she asked slyly.

"Oh, don't you start too, Laurie!" Alecia cried. "I already told Monica and Connor that I don't want to go." Just the thought made her feel queasy.

"It'll be so fun! You have to come. It won't be any fun if you don't."

"I don't want to talk about it, okay?" Alecia said. She shoved her jacket inside her bag and dropped it on the bench beside her. Stacie and the others got up and went to help Jeremy bring in the nets.

"You're such a chicken! I bet you can't dance, that's probably why you won't go," Laurie teased. Alecia opened her mouth to answer, but before she could say anything Lexi appeared and sat down beside her.

Alecia looked over at Lexi, noticing the red-rimmed eyes and angry scowl. Had Lexi been crying? she wondered. She glanced at Laurie, who raised her eyebrows at Alecia.

"Are you okay, Lexi?" Laurie asked gently.

"I'm fine," Lexi snapped, turning away from Alecia and Laurie.

"Are you sure?" Laurie asked, moving from the floor to the bench beside Lexi. "You look upset."

"Well, I'm fine. But thanks for asking," Lexi muttered and turned away.

"Okay, if you say so," Laurie agreed. "You played well last weekend. It was a good game," Laurie said. Lexi fussed with her pads, not looking at Laurie. "Do your parents come out to watch you play sometimes? I know I always play way better when mine are watching, kind of like I'm showing off or something."

"Why don't you just mind your own business? Huh? Being a good captain doesn't mean sticking your nose where it doesn't belong!" Lexi cried, her voice rising so that almost the whole room could hear her. "Just leave me alone!"

Laurie got up from the bench and walked quickly away but not before Alecia caught the stricken look on her face. She went after her and caught Laurie's arm. "Don't let her bother you, Laurie," she whispered. "She just had a fight with her dad. That's probably what's got her upset. It isn't you," she said, rubbing the girl's arm. Laurie smiled weakly at Alecia.

"Yeah, I guess I shouldn't take it too personally," she said, but Alecia could tell she did.

Alecia found herself paired with Lexi for a one-on-one exercise. Normally Alecia wouldn't have minded. Lexi was a good player, skilled and quick. She had a good eye and read situations well. But tonight Lexi was in a bad mood and nothing Alecia did pleased her. Even at the best of times she liked to point out mistakes and tell people how to correct them, but tonight it was even worse. Finally Alecia sat on the floor and leaned against the gym wall, fed up.

"What are you doing?" Lexi cried, trapping the ball with her foot. She put her hands on her hips and glared at Alecia. "We aren't finished."

"Well, I am," Alecia told heir, scowling. "I'm tired of you telling me how terrible a player I am."

"You aren't even trying," Lexi accused her. Alecia started to defend herself but before she could say anything Jeremy had come over. He stood looking at the two girls.

"Alecia, why aren't you playing?" he asked.

"I'm tired of Lexi criticizing everything I do," she told him. "I'm too slow, I'm too easy, I'm not paying attention, I'm offside, blah, blah, blah."

"Lexi, let's just concentrate on our own play, okay?"

Jeremy said, turning to her. "Alecia will play better if she isn't constantly worrying about what she's doing wrong. Now, let's get on with it, please, girls."

Alecia stood up slowly, eyeing Lexi carefully. The other girl threw her a scornful glance and shook her head. "Once again the team princess is rescued by daddy," she said under her breath.

"What's that supposed to mean?" Alecia asked, flushing and suddenly angry.

"You always think you're something special around here because your daddy is the coach. I hate people like that."

The nasty retort that sprang to Alecia's lips was cut off as Jeremy blew his whistle, ending the drill. Lexi walked away without another word, leaving Alecia standing alone. Her pulse was racing and her hand shook as she lifted it to push her bangs out of her eyes. Was it true? Did she take advantage of the situation? She didn't think so. She was always very aware of the fact that Jeremy was her stepfather. She had never wanted the other girls to think of her as any different from them. But now Lexi had made her doubt herself. Maybe if Lexi thought that way, they all did.

7 OFFSIDE!

It wasn't the best practice they'd ever had and Alecia was glad when the night was over. The girls gathered around the benches collecting gear and getting ready to leave. Alecia took off her shin pads and shoved them in her bag, then threw in her empty water bottle after them. Grabbing the mesh bag of soccer balls, she headed outside to wait for Jeremy in the car.

She threw the balls in the trunk and turned to see Lexi heading out of the parking lot alone. So her father hadn't shown up after all, Alecia thought, and felt a twinge of sympathy for the girl. She wouldn't have wanted to walk home in the dark. The neighbourhood was a fairly nice one, but you could never be sure. Alecia knew, however, that Lexi wouldn't accept a ride from Jeremy, so she said nothing as he came outside and joined her at the car.

"All set?" he asked as he opened his door. Alecia nodded silently and slipped inside. "You and Lexi seemed to be having some trouble getting along tonight. Do you want to talk about it?" he asked as they drove out of the parking lot.

For a second Alecia thought about brushing it off. She didn't want Jeremy going and talking to Lexi about it. That would just make things worse. But then, she always talked to her parents about what was bothering her. She wasn't very good at keeping it all bottled up inside.

"She said I get special treatment because you're my dad. She called me the team princess and said she hates people like me. I don't, do I? Get special treatment?" Alecia asked.

"Of course not. I treat you all the same. You know that."

"I guess," Alecia said, looking out the window. "It's not even true," she went on, more to herself than to Jeremy.

"What's not true?"

"You're not even my dad. She kept calling you my 'daddy.' But you're not."

Jeremy cleared his throat. "You know, I consider myself your father," he said slowly.

"You do?"

"Certainly. I love you. I care about what happens to you. Aren't those things that fathers feel?"

"Yeah, I guess. But it's just because I'm there, you know. Mom and I came as a package. You didn't really have a choice, if you wanted to be with my mom."

"It started out that way, certainly. But I've known you since you were a little girl, Leesh. And long ago I loved you for yourself, not because of your mother. If something were to happen to your mom I would raise you as my daughter. That is the way I feel."

Alecia said nothing. This was all so strange and new and slightly scary. She glanced at Jeremy, studying him, wondering. She guessed she had known that he loved her. She loved him too. He was a great guy. But she didn't consider him her father. She already had one of those, she thought, thinking of the scrapbook, of the journal with its first tentative entries, fiercely guarded, lying between her mattress and box spring.

★ ★ ★

Sunday morning dawned wet and cold. Alecia looked hopefully at Jeremy during breakfast. She thought maybe he'd have a heart and cancel the game due to bad weather, but no such luck.

"I should have taken up swimming," Alecia grumbled as they headed for the field. The windshield wipers were going full speed and the sky was one solid mass of thick grey clouds.

"You'd sink," Jeremy reminded her.

"I could learn! I think I'll learn to swim this summer. I really should know how, since we live so close to water. Mom has been very negligent in that area,"

Alecia said, scowling out the window. She had plastic bags under her jersey, but she knew it would take only seconds for the rest of her to be soaked right through. Vancouverites were strange people, she thought, forcing their children to play outside in bad weather.

The rest of the Burrards arrived grumbling and scowling at the sky as well, but Jeremy was blind and deaf to their complaints. He got them running their warm-up and doing their stretches and after a while the grumbling had mostly stopped. They were playing the Spitfires — a team they frequently beat — so everyone was optimistic that if it was going to be a wet game, it would at least be a victorious one.

The referee blew the whistle calling the players to their positions, and the Burrards quickly ran out. Alecia was not on the field for the first bit so she sat on the bench, her raincoat pulled tightly around her, trying to stay somewhat dry as long as possible.

The game started off okay, but quickly deteriorated as the field got muddier and muddier. Girls attempting to kick the ball slipped, ending up on their rears. Players trying to complete checks ended up on their faces in the mud. By halftime both teams were nearly unrecognizable. Alecia glanced down at herself in dismay. She hated being dirty, hated the feeling of mud on her skin. She seethed inside, but said nothing, knowing she would get no sympathy anyway. The only good thing about the morning was that it had finally stopped raining.

Her mother had packed hot chocolate in a thermos for her and she sipped it thankfully at the bench during halftime. So far they were deadlocked at zero. It was better than being behind, but not good enough. Everyone was crabby and cold and sore. Stacie had ugly red welts on her legs from where the wet ball had smacked her and Marnie had gone home with what Jeremy suspected was a sprained wrist. They were a mess.

"I hope time speeds up," Laurie whispered, coming to sit with Alecia on the bench. "I don't think I can manage another twenty minutes of this torture."

"It would help if we could at least score a goal," Alecia said, glancing across the field at the Spitfire bench. They were just as sorry looking as the Burrards.

"Yeah well, I'm trying," Laurie snapped. Alecia glanced at her in surprise. Laurie never snapped.

"What's wrong?" she asked. "I mean besides the obvious."

"Oh, that Lexi," Laurie said, shaking her head. "I've got to stop letting her bug me, I really do. But sometimes."

"What'd she do this time?"

"Same old thing. Telling me in a hundred different ways that I'm not a good captain. Just before the last throw-in she told me it was my fault the ball had gone out of bounds. She said she saw me kick it out deliberately." Laurie was staring at the ground, her shoulders hunched. She didn't say anything else and Alecia didn't know what to say to make her feel better. She glanced around the field idly, stopping when she spotted Lexi, talking to a man. With them were a woman and a little boy. Alecia nudged Laurie, who looked up to where Alecia was pointing.

"Is that Lexi's family?" Laurie asked, squinting at the little group.

"I guess so. I've never met her father."

"Is that her mother, then?" Laurie asked, "and little brother? He sure is cute."

They watched as Lexi knelt down in front of the boy, refastening his raincoat snaps. He grinned at her and threw his arms around her neck.

"I don't think so," Alecia said. "I think her name is Brenda or something. Her stepmom, I guess. I don't really know."

Alecia and Laurie were quiet as Lexi and her family approached the rest of the team. Lexi ignored the girls and headed directly for Jeremy.

"Well, Jeremy Parker," Mr. Thomas said, holding out his hand to shake Jeremy's. "How long has it been?" He was smiling, nodding, friendly. Not like Thursday night.

"This is my wife, Brenda, and our son, Scott," Lexi's dad said, turning to his wife. "Brenda, this is the guy I was telling you about, Jeremy Parker. He was kind enough to allow Alexandra to play on his team."

Jeremy and Mr. Thomas chatted until the referee blew the whistle ending the break. They shook hands again, promising to get in touch, then Lexi's father put an arm around his wife and they started to walk away.

Lexi ran after them. "Aren't you going to stay to watch the second half?" she asked.

"It hasn't been all that exciting so far, Alexandra," her father told her. "You girls need to get some offence going, create opportunity. We'll stay a couple more minutes. But it's wet and Scott is getting bored."

"Scott likes to watch me play, don't you?" Lexi asked, bending down to the little boy. He grinned at her, his face round and shiny beneath his rain hat.

"He has to have his nap, Alexandra," Brenda said shortly, taking Scott's hand. "We can't stay too much longer."

The referee blew his whistle to start the second half and the girls slowly made their way back onto the field. Alecia headed for her position on the field too, making her way through the mess of chewed-up grass and mud. Although it had stopped raining, it was too late as far as the field was concerned. She glanced over at Lexi as the girl took up her position. She caught Alecia's eye and glared at her. Alecia looked away. Alecia didn't care how unpleasant her stepmother was, Lexi didn't need to treat her teammates the way she did. It would be easier to like her if she'd just be a little nicer sometimes.

The second half began hard and fast. Both teams seemed determined to score that first goal. Early on, Alecia received a pass from Laurie and dribbled up the middle, keeping two opposing forwards from the ball. It was tricky, keeping her feet moving, controlling the ball, and trying not to slip on the slick playing surface. Shielding the ball from the Spitfires' centre, who was kicking at it between Alecia's legs, she glanced up for someone to pass to and caught sight of Lexi, waiting just to her left. Alecia held up her hand, then kicked wildly in Lexi's direction. Lexi caught the pass, lost it, regained it, and shot at the net. The ball headed straight for the goalkeeper's outstretched arms, but bounced just in front of her, spraying mud into her face. The goalkeeper sputtered, trying to keep her eye on the ball, but she couldn't see it and it rolled slowly until it sat, finally, in a puddle just over the line.

"Way to go!" everyone screamed, forgetting that they disliked Lexi as they tackled her. Lexi tolerated it for a few seconds then broke away, scanning the sidelines eagerly. Alecia, standing just beside her, guessed she was looking for her father, but he wasn't there. There was no one on the sidelines except Jeremy and the Burrards who weren't on the field. Lexi's shoulders slumped and she kicked at a piece of sod, sending it flying.

Suddenly, Alecia felt sorry for her. If Lexi's family had stayed just a few minutes longer they would have seen her goal. Alecia knew how much it meant to her when her own mom saw her do well on the field. She cleared her throat and approached Lexi cautiously.

"That was a great goal, Lexi," she said. The girl

looked up and stared at Alecia for a second without answering. Then she shrugged slightly and kicked at the ground again.

"Thanks."

"Too bad your dad missed it," Alecia went on.

"What's that supposed to mean? Huh? Why don't you just mind your own business?" Lexi cried, one hand clenching into a fist. Alecia took a step back, frightened that Lexi would hit her. Thankfully, the whistle blew and the ball was thrown into play again.

Laurie passed to Lexi, who bolted upfield like she'd been shot out of a gun. She passed cross-field to Allison, who dribbled forward a few feet before the ball was stolen from her and play returned the other way. Lexi got in tight with the Spitfire centre and the two girls fought hard for the ball. It was finally kicked free and three players were right there, ready to pounce on it. Alecia took an elbow in her right side, which winded her slightly, but she kept with it and managed to come up with the ball. She ran with it, then dropped it behind her for Laurie. The Burrards' captain took over and gained the centre line with no one near her. But the whistle blew and the referee pointed at Lexi, indicating that she was offside.

Lexi blew up. "I was not!" she screamed at the ref. "I was not offside!" she replied, following the man, who ignored her.

"Listen to me, darn it!" Lexi cried, grabbing at the

man's arm. "I was not offside! I know what offside looks like and I was in after the ball. You need your eyes examined!" she said, her face red. Alecia and the other Burrards stared in utter disbelief at Lexi. Laurie made her way over, slowly, obviously reluctant to get involved. She and Jeremy arrived at the same time. Lexi spun on them, her hands clenched into fists, her breathing laboured.

"Tell this jerk I was not offside. He wasn't paying attention!" she cried at Jeremy.

"Take your player off the field, coach," the ref said quietly to Jeremy.

"No! I will not get off the field! You can't just call stuff 'cause you feel like it! I was not offside! I will not leave the field. I didn't do anything. You stopped a perfectly good scoring chance! Laurie would have scored!" Lexi continued, tears streaming down her dirty cheeks.

"Take your player off the field now, coach, or I will forfeit the game to the other side. And she's out of the game."

"Let's go, Lexi," Jeremy said calmly, taking Lexi by the arm. Lexi seemed to collapse at his touch. She stopped screaming and let herself be led to the bench. The whistle blew and the girls on the field had to pull their attention back to the game. No one said anything and no one saw Lexi leave.

The game ended in a tie with the Spitfires scoring with only three minutes left. The Burrards didn't even care by that point. They were tired and dirty and stunned. No one had ever seen a player blow up at a referee like that before, although their old coach had done it many times.

"What was with her?" Stacie asked. Her face was completely painted in mud, the whites of her eyes and her teeth the only colour showing. Alecia tried not to giggle, knowing she wasn't much prettier.

"I think she was upset because her dad missed seeing her goal. He left before she scored," she said.

"That's it? My parents have missed most of my goals," Allison said, her voice scornful. "And she was offside, no matter what she says."

"Lexi is always offside," Stacie muttered and a couple of the girls laughed. "Well, she is! She's always going where she shouldn't, always saying things she shouldn't. I don't know how she figures after two weeks that she has the right to tell the rest of us how to play, or Laurie how to be captain."

"Well," Laurie began, "maybe she is all those things, does those things. But she was still upset today. We all get upset sometimes. Even me." Laurie looked around at the group, smiling. Stacie knocked against her shoulder, laughing, and the others joined in. It was hard to imagine easygoing Laurie getting upset.

The field cleared quickly and Alecia was grateful for the warm, dry car when she finally climbed in. She leaned against the headrest and closed her eyes, thinking of the nasty scene on the field. Then her thoughts wandered to the scene between Lexi and her family. What was with them? she wondered. Didn't they like Lexi? And where was her own mother?

"Why doesn't Lexi live with her mom anymore?" she asked, breaking the silence of the car. Jeremy glanced at her, surprised.

"I don't know, Alecia," he said, turning back to the road. "You would have to ask Lexi."

Alecia grunted. Ask and get yelled at? she thought. Not likely. She leaned back against her seat and closed her eyes, putting Lexi and her problems out of her mind.

8 JEREMY SPEAKS

Alecia sat at her desk staring blankly at the page before her. She had lots of work to keep her busy but somehow she couldn't concentrate. She'd taken a long, hot shower when she got home from the soccer game and put on her warmest, comfiest clothes, but she still felt restless and bored. Finally she tossed her pencil on the desk and wandered downstairs. Her mother and Jeremy were in the den where Jeremy was working at the computer and her mother was curled in the easy chair reading a book. She smiled as Alecia wandered into the room.

"Hi sweetie, what's up?" she asked, putting her book aside.

"Oh, just feeling a bit restless I guess," Alecia told her, perching on the edge of the chair. "Maybe it's the weather." And that game, she thought, shuddering.

"The weather around this city has that effect on people in January, that's for sure," Jeremy agreed, looking up from the keyboard. "Maybe we should all go for a walk," he suggested hopefully.

Alecia and her mother looked at each other and laughed. "Yeah right, Jeremy," Alecia said. "Haven't you had enough of the outdoors for one day? I think I'm growing webbing between my toes after this morning."

"It would clear the cobwebs out of your brains," he said, trying again.

"Actually," Mrs. Parker said, closing her book and standing up, "I have a couple of errands to run and I may as well do them now." She kissed Alecia. "I'll leave you two alone, if that's okay," she said, glancing at Jeremy. They raised their eyebrows at each other in a silent sentence. Alecia glanced from one to the other. She got the feeling she was being set up, but wasn't exactly sure how. She was pretty sure she hadn't done anything wrong in the last couple of days. Was it something to do with soccer? she wondered. That could be it. Maybe Jeremy wanted to talk to her about Lexi. Well, she wasn't the one being miserable and nasty all the time. That was Lexi. And if Jeremy wanted her to try and be more of a leader on the team, then she would just remind him of his promise not to expect any more from her than from the rest of the girls.

Alecia was so wrapped up in her defensive strategies, she didn't realize her mother was long gone and that Jeremy had shut off the computer and was standing in front of her.

"How 'bout some lunch?" he offered, holding out

his hand to her. She frowned at him, suspicious, but took the offered hand and followed him into the kitchen. She perched on a chair while Jeremy pulled out bread and jam and peanut butter. The sandwich maker he had received for Christmas made incredible toasted peanut butter and grape jelly sandwiches. All her friends wanted them when they came over.

"This okay?" Jeremy asked, holding up the jar of peanut butter.

"Do you have to ask?" Alecia teased, grinning.

Jeremy brought the finished sandwiches to the table along with the milk jug and two glasses, then sat beside Alecia. They ate in silence for a few minutes, the only sound in the room was their chewing and swallowing. Alecia waited. She knew he wanted to talk to her about something. She just wished she could figure out what it was.

"Alecia," Jeremy said finally, wiping his mouth with a napkin. He pushed his plate away from him and leaned forward in his chair, looking at her with his serious face. The one he used when he was explaining math stuff, or talking about a play in soccer. "Alecia, there is something I've been thinking of for quite a while now. For several months, actually, and I've made up my mind that the best thing to do is just to talk to you about it and see what you think. How you feel."

"I agree," Alecia said, popping the last of her sandwich into her mouth. "Whatever it is, the answer is definitely maybe."

"I'm serious, Alecia," he said. The fact that he kept using her full name instead of her nickname, which is what he usually called her, was setting Alecia on edge. Was her mother sick?

"Okay," she mumbled, crossing her arms and staring at him.

"What would you think of my adopting you legally, making you my daughter?" Jeremy asked.

The words spun around in Alecia's head until they became all mixed up and she wasn't sure she had even heard him correctly. "Your daughter?" she parroted, frowning at him.

"Yes. I want to make you my daughter. I've been thinking about it for a long time, but your mother said I should wait. Wait until we'd had a chance to live together and get to know each other as a family. I know you've been thinking a lot about your dad, wondering about him. And I know it is natural for teenagers to think about who they are and where they belong. I want you to belong to me. I want the three of us to be a complete family. For you to be my daughter. To share my name."

"But I have a name," Alecia whispered. She felt as though a tidal wave had swept over her and was washing her out to sea.

"You're right, you do. And I would never try and take that away from you. You could have both names if that was what you wanted. But I feel like I am your father in the true sense of the word. I want for us to make it legal."

"Would you want me to call you Dad?" she asked from beneath the roaring.

Jeremy chuckled softly and shook his head. "You could call me anything you want, as long as it was polite," he told her gently. He reached out a hand and took Alecia's, holding it firmly. "This is a big question and I can see I've completely overwhelmed you. Maybe scared you a bit. I want you to think about this for as long as you need to. Talk to your mom, talk to your friends. You could even see a counsellor if you want. You come back to me when you are ready to make a decision one way or the other. And listen, Alecia," he said and paused, looking at her carefully, "if the answer is no, it won't change how I feel about you, or what I think of you. Do you understand that? I mean it. This is your decision to make and I will respect your choice."

"Yeah, okay," Alecia said, nodding. She pulled her hand from Jeremy's and wandered out of the room and up the stairs.

She lay on her bed, staring at the photograph of herself and her parents, feeling the scrapbook beneath her. She supposed she should have seen it coming, this request. But she hadn't. And she wasn't sure what to do with it. What did she want? Didn't she already have a dad? Wasn't he right there in the picture, smiling at her? Wasn't Peter Sheffield still her father? Isn't that what she wanted?

Alecia picked up the silver frame and studied the photo carefully. She looked like her father. Even her mother had said so. They had the same face shape, and their eyes were the same colour, a mossy shade of green. Dad's hair had been dark brown, not blond, but it was straight like Alecia's and her mother had told her that her laugh was very much like her dad's.

He had missed so much of her life in the past nine years. She was trying to give some of it back to him in her notes. She was sure he had been upset about the wedding, upset at all the games he had missed watching her play, all the school concerts and report cards. How could she hurt him yet again by letting Jeremy adopt her? Adopt her as though there were no one else with any claim to her.

Her mother had told her once that her father would be glad to know that they had moved on with their lives. He wanted for them to be happy and Jeremy made her mother happy. Jeremy made Alecia happy. They were a family. But still, Alecia had this pull, this tie with the past that had nothing to do with Jeremy. And she wasn't sure she wanted to let go of it. She didn't want a new dad. She wanted the one she had lost.

Alecia put the photo back on her bedside table and rolled over to face the wall. Her eyes stung and her throat felt tight and sore. She shoved her hands between her bent knees and squeezed her eyes shut. What Jeremy was asking her to do was too hard. She didn't think she could do it.

What seemed like hours later she heard the phone ring and then Jeremy's voice calling up the stairs. It was Connor.

"Hey, what's up?" he asked when she got to the phone.

"Not much, I guess. Just hanging out." Alecia didn't really feel like talking. She just wanted to hide in her room, alone.

"Want to come over for awhile? I've got a new game for the Wii."

"I thought Laurie made you give those things up," Alecia said, smiling despite herself. Connor knew her weakness for video games. He always beat her, always, but she was a sucker for punishment.

"Ah, what Laurie doesn't know won't hurt her, right? Besides, I haven't seen you in ages and I'm lonely."

"So you want me to keep you from being bored? Is that it? I'm guessing Laurie is unable to entertain you."

"Are you coming over or not?" Connor demanded, ignoring Alecia's comments.

"Give me ten minutes," she said and quickly hung up. Maybe spending a couple of hours with Connor would help pull her out of her strange mood.

An hour later she was perched on the edge of her seat in Connor's family room, controller in hand, battling fierce alien warriors. She and Connor hadn't done this in months, she realized. She was surprised at how much she had missed it. Her bad mood had completely disappeared.

"Ha ha! Take that, you villian!" Connor cried, his body twisting and turning as he steered his ship. "No! Watch out, Leesh, watch out!"

Alecia threw her controller down in defeat and lay back on the pillows to watch Connor. It didn't take long before his ship exploded into a fiery ball as well. "Where do you find these awful games?" Alecia asked, stifling a yawn. "They're awfully bloodthirsty."

"Yeah, isn't it great?" Connor said, grinning. "Dad and I play together. He's much better at it than I am. Gillian is terrible. She always gets upset when she dies," he said, standing suddenly. "Hey, you hungry? Want something to eat? How about a sandwich?"

"As long as it isn't tuna. I hate tuna," Alecia said, following him into the kitchen.

She sat at the counter and watched as Connor pulled stuff from the fridge. She loved the Stevens' house. It was much bigger and newer than her own, and beautifully decorated.

"So, how is it?" Connor asked, watching as Alecia took a first, hesitant bite. You never knew with Connor. Sometimes his creations could be a little wild.

"It's good. Thanks."

They were still eating when Connor's dad wandered in from the garage. He had on a pair of very dirty coveralls and was wiping his hands on an even grimier rag. He smiled at the two of them.

"Hello Alecia. I haven't seen you in ages," he said.

"That's because Connor never invites me over now that he has a girlfriend," she said, glancing slyly at her friend. Connor stuck his tongue out at her.

"Around here we don't mind so much. Keeps him out of our hair," his father said. He stood beside Connor, one hand on his son's shoulder. He kept looking at Alecia, talking casually, but very quickly his other hand shot out and snatched the pickle from Connor's plate. It happened so fast, Connor didn't even notice. Alecia grinned as Connor suddenly realized what had happened.

"Get your hands off my food, old man!" he cried, covering the remains of his snack with his hands.

"Watch who you are calling old, little boy."

Alecia sat quietly, enjoying the easy bantering between her friend and his dad. They seemed like such good friends, rather than just father and son.

"Hey, did I tell you about the fishing trip me and Dad are taking in June? Kind of a Father's Day/birthday type thing. Just the two of us for four days. Skipping out of school and everything," Connor said. Alecia smiled as he described where they would be staying, what kind of fishing they would try. He positively glowed with excitement.

Would her own father have taken Alecia fishing? Had he even liked to fish? An image of two people in a boat appeared before her. They were sitting in the middle of the lake with fishing rods in their hands and they looked happy. The sun was shining, it was very quiet. Alecia smiled to herself, enjoying the picture. Just her and her dad. Except, she realized suddenly, the man in the boat with her wasn't Peter Sheffield. It was Jeremy. Alecia blinked and gazed around the kitchen. Connor and his dad were still talking about their plans. She sighed. She would never get to go fishing with her dad. She wouldn't ever get to do anything with him.

"I think I'll get going, Connor," she said abruptly, sliding from her stool. She put her dishes in the sink and left the kitchen. She was pulling on her boots when Connor came out and stood beside her.

"Everything okay, Leesh?" he asked. She looked up at his concerned face and tried to smile.

"Sure. Thanks for the snack and games. Next time I'll beat you," she said, trying to sound more normal. She opened the door, but stood for another second, struggling with the zipper on her jacket.

Connor looked at her a little longer, not quite believing her, but then he shrugged. "No problem. Anytime. I get tired of being active sometimes — you know how it is."

"Yeah, that Laurie, she really keeps you hopping." The two friends grinned at each other and then Alecia waved and headed off down the walkway.

9 MORE TROUBLE

Alecia was still sitting at the dinner table Tuesday night when Jeremy came downstairs wearing his tracksuit, his whistle hanging from his neck. He frowned at her.

"We have to go, Leesh," he said.

"Yeah," Alecia agreed, but made no move to get up from the table. The knot in her stomach made her feel sick and she wondered if she was maybe getting the stomach flu. She hoped so.

"Are you planning to get ready?" Jeremy asked, tossing his water bottle into his gym bag.

"The thing is," Alecia began, "I'm not feeling all that well. Maybe I should just stay home tonight."

"This not feeling well wouldn't have anything to do with Lexi would it?"

"I don't know. My stomach hurts. I feel like I'm going to be sick."

"You'll have a break Thursday," he said. "I have to cancel practice. And I'll have a talk with everyone at the start of practice, and maybe a private one with Lexi.

But you can't hide from the situation, Leesh. You have to face it."

"If I puke on the gym floor you have to clean it up," Alecia reminded him.

"Come with me. If you still feel like you're going to be sick once we start practising, I'll let you sit out."

"You're a heartless man," Alecia told him, pushing herself from the table.

"So I've heard."

★ ★ ★

The drills were hard that night — Jeremy worked them constantly, with little break in between. They did a lot of running and passing, a lot of blocking and checking. It was good, actually, Alecia decided, wiping her hand across her sweaty forehead. It was good to get her heart pounding and her adrenalin pumping. She could tell the others felt the same way. All of their frustrations and stresses were being pounded out on the gym floor. Even Lexi was working hard, paying close attention to the drills and not saying much to the other girls.

It seemed as though the practice would be a good one, until about halfway through. Alecia wasn't anywhere near the others when the trouble started. In fact she was across the gym working with Allison when the yelling started. Everyone in the room stopped and turned in the direction of the voices. Alecia glanced around but Jeremy didn't seem to be in the room just then.

"You stupid idiot!" Lexi cried. "Why don't you pay attention to what is going on? You could have killed me!" She was screaming at Stacie, the ball held tight in her arms.

Stacie's face was red, every muscle in her body tensed. "Why don't you keep your head up?" she asked.

"I was paying attention. You think you can just do whatever the heck you want to. You and just about everyone else on this stupid team!"

"What's the problem here?" Laurie asked, joining the two players.

"Mind your own business, Laurie," Lexi said, turning her back on the captain. "This has nothing to do with you."

"This twit kicks the ball on net, then gets smacked in the back when I kick it out again. Now she's saying I'm not paying attention. Who wasn't paying attention, *Alexandra*?" Stacie said.

"Stacie, come on, don't make things worse," Laurie said. "Lexi, you have to watch out for Stacie. She doesn't like to smother the ball. She keeps it in play. Don't turn your back on her." Laurie spoke calmly, her tone appeasing. But Lexi didn't buy it. She turned on Laurie, furious.

"Don't tell me what to do!" she cried. "You think all there is to being a captain is patting everyone on the back and telling them to be a good girl? You have to lead a team, not coddle them along. Who made you captain, anyway? Huh? Whoever it was needs to have their head examined!" Lexi cried as Jeremy swung the door open and came back inside.

"What's going on here, girls?" he asked, setting the cones on the floor. No one said anything and the only sound in the room was the heavy breathing.

"This is the second practice in a row where there have been raised voices and angry faces. If no one is going to tell me why, then perhaps we'll just knock off early tonight. We have a game Sunday, an important one, and if this is the attitude we're taking into it, we're going to lose."

"Sorry, Jeremy," Stacie muttered. "It'll be okay now."

"Lexi?" Jeremy asked, turning to look at the girl.

"Whatever," Lexi said, still scowling.

"You girls better figure out a way to get along. This is getting silly," Jeremy told them. He ended practice a few minutes later. Everyone was just as glad to be finished and the gym cleared quickly.

★ ★ ★

Laurie called Wednesday night. Alecia took the call in her mother's bedroom, curled up on the bed in her usual fashion. Laurie got right to the point.

"I'm calling to tell you I resign as captain. Would you tell Jeremy for me?" she asked.

"What?" Alecia cried. "You can't quit, Laurie! We need you."

"I'm sorry, Leesh," Laurie said, sounding close to tears. "I can't do it anymore. I can't handle Lexi's criticism. Maybe I am a bad captain. Stacie might be better. Or someone else. I'm not very good at fights."

"You can't let Lexi win, Laurie! That's what she wants, for you to quit. Besides, there's no one else to take over. You know Stacie would be a lousy captain. Please, Laurie, you can't quit."

"I won't quit, Leesh. I love soccer. I just don't want to be captain anymore. Please, would you tell Jeremy for me? I know I should tell him myself, but I'm kind of chicken. I don't want him to try and talk me out of it."

"Laurie, please don't do anything just yet. We can work something out. I'll talk to Jeremy, tell him he has to do something about Lexi."

"I've already decided, Leesh. Just promise me you'll tell Jeremy."

Alecia clenched her jaw. She liked Laurie an awful lot, but she wasn't going to make it easy for her to quit as captain. "I wish you'd rethink this, Laurie, but if you won't you're going to have to tell Jeremy yourself."

Laurie said nothing although Alecia could hear her breathing. After a long second she sighed. "I guess you're right. I should do it myself. Is he there? Can you get him for me?" she asked.

Alecia hung around outside Jeremy's office while he talked to Laurie. Her stomach was all tied up in knots and she kept twisting her fingers around themselves.

What would Jeremy do? Would he be able to convince her to change her mind? Alecia remembered the previous fall when Anne had called to tell Jeremy she quit. She hadn't wanted to hear that information either.

Eventually Jeremy hung up the phone and came to stand in the doorway. He gazed at Alecia, his eyes solemn behind their glasses. "This is getting ridiculous, Leesh," he said.

"Yeah," Alecia agreed.

"You girls have got to figure out a way of getting along. And now you have to figure out who will replace Laurie as captain." He stared at her for another couple of seconds, then shook his head and went back in the office.

Alecia watched him leave then went back to her room. She sat at her desk and stared at the books lying there. What would happen when her team found out that Lexi had chased away their popular captain? And who would replace Laurie? She shivered, though the room wasn't all that cold, and wrapped her arms around herself. Everything was getting so complicated and ugly.

★ ★ ★

"Where's Monica today?" Alecia asked Friday afternoon as she and Anne pushed through the heavy orange fire doors. It had been a long, tiring week. Alecia had tried to talk to Laurie again, but Laurie had kept to herself, obviously not wanting to talk. Alecia understood, but she was frustrated and upset. Alecia was afraid the whole team would collapse if something didn't happen. Still, Jeremy seemed determined not to ask Lexi to leave. He insisted they all needed to figure out a way to get along. Alecia was glad the week was over, but Sunday's game was looming closer and closer and she shuddered every time she thought of it.

"Oh, some appointment or something," Anne said, her voice low, distracted. They left the school grounds and headed along the sidewalk, walking slowly in the cool February afternoon. The sun had come out, but it had no warmth. Alecia couldn't wait for spring. She was so tired of bulky sweaters and thick coats. She wanted to wear her pretty clothes again. She glanced at her friend, wondering what was up. Anne wasn't usually so quiet and withdrawn.

"What's going on?" she asked finally, when Anne didn't say anything. "Something happen at school today?"

"Oh, Alecia," Anne cried, wringing her hands together. "I've been trying to decide whether to say anything to you or not. I just don't know what to do!"

"Is it about Lexi and soccer?" Alecia asked. She had never seen Anne so upset. Her friend nodded miserably. "Well, you should probably tell me. I don't know what else there could be to know, though. Laurie quitting was pretty bad." Alecia had filled Anne in on her conversation with Laurie. Like Alecia, Anne couldn't believe it had come to that. Now it looked like there was even more trouble.

"After gym, when we were changing, I overheard a couple of girls talking," Anne began, speaking slowly. "They were talking about the Burrards, Leesh. There is going to be a boycott this weekend."

"A boycott?" Alecia repeated, stupidly. Her brain was fuzzy and she was having difficulty concentrating on Anne's words. "A boycott of what?"

"The game, Alecia. The team is going to boycott the game against the Rocketeers. They are going to refuse to play with Lexi." Anne looked as though she were ready to cry. Alecia stared at her.

"How did they find out?" she asked finally.

"I'm not sure, really," Anne told her. "Somehow one of the girls I heard talking must have overheard it somewhere."

"Maybe it isn't really true," Alecia said, but she knew it was. She looked at Anne.

"What are you going to do? They're going to throw the game!" her friend said, touching her arm.

"I know, Annie. What am I supposed to do? They didn't want me to know, obviously. Maybe I should just pretend like I don't know. Maybe that is the best thing."

"But if Jeremy knows ahead of time, maybe he can change their minds," Anne suggested.

Alecia felt as though everything that had happened in the last week, right from when Jeremy had asked to adopt her to this very second, was weighing down on her. Like Atlas, she was holding the weight of the world on her shoulders. And it was way, way too heavy.

10 TAKING A STAND

Dear Dad,

Things are pretty terrible around here right now. One of the girls on our soccer team is really upsetting everyone else. She even made our captain quit. And now the rest of the girls want to boycott an important game this Sunday! I only found out because Anne overheard some girls at school talking about it and told me. They didn't want me to know. Now I don't know whether I should tell Jeremy or not. What would you do? Would you want to know? I don't want to betray my teammates, but I don't want to betray Jeremy either. He's a great coach. I'm so confused. I wish things could just go back to the way they used to be before Lexi came. I don't understand why she is so nasty all the time. Jeremy says there is probably a reason, but I don't know what it is. I think she's just like that. I wish you could help me. I really need you.

Love, Alecia

★ ★ ★

Sunday morning was sunny and bright. Alecia woke up and lay in bed, her stomach churning. She had done nothing. Nothing at all. Just kept her mouth shut, telling herself she couldn't make up her mind what to do. And now it was too late. Jeremy was downstairs in his coaching clothes, eating his toast and drinking a cup of coffee. He assumed there would be a team of players at the field waiting for him. Waiting to play.

Alecia rolled over and stared at the wall. She hadn't slept well the night before. She felt heavy and foggy. Could she pretend to be sick? Pretend that she couldn't play? Not a chance. Jeremy always saw right through her. He'd never let her off. She got up and pulled on her uniform. The clothes hurt her skin. She braided her hair and scowled at herself in the mirror. She was a traitor no matter what she did. She couldn't win, and for a second she really hated Stacie and the others for putting her in such an awkward position. It wasn't fair. She hadn't done anything wrong. She wasn't the one tearing the team apart.

"Let's get it moving, Leesh!" Jeremy called up and Alecia went slowly down the stairs, her feet like lead weights at the ends of her legs. It was a good thing there wasn't going to be a game today, she decided, since she could barely walk, let alone run.

They arrived at the field, the same one as the week

before, and Jeremy took his time getting the practice balls out of the car and over to their side of the field. Alecia followed along behind him slowly. There were girls already there, huddled together, watching Alecia and Jeremy make their way across the field. Alecia didn't see Lexi, but that didn't mean anything — she was usually late.

"Morning, ladies," Jeremy called out as he passed them, waving. Alecia stopped at the outskirts of the group, unsure of herself.

"Hey, Leesh," Stacie said.

"Talk them out of it, Leesh," Nancy said, grabbing Alecia's arm. "They figure it's going to help. That it's actually going to change things, instead of making them worse."

Alecia swallowed hard and decided to play dumb. "What are you talking about?" she whispered.

"They're not going to play!" Nancy cried, then lowered her voice. "They are going to tell Jeremy they won't play in today's game if he lets Lexi play. They're going to boycott the game."

"We have to do this, Leesh," Stacie said firmly, her eyes cold. "I know Jeremy's your stepdad and everything, but we have to let him know how we feel."

Alecia was suddenly very angry. Angry at Lexi, for starting all this nonsense, but angry at Stacie, too, and the others who agreed with her. What did they think was going to happen?

"He could quit, Stace," she said, her voice shaking.

"I doubt it. But we'll take our chances, right girls?" Stacie asked, scanning the team. Just about every girl nodded in agreement. It seemed Nancy was a minority.

"Here's Laurie," someone said.

Stacie pulled Laurie aside and filled her in. Alecia saw Laurie go white as Stacie spoke and she shook her head hard, her black hair smacking her face.

"No! Don't you dare!" she cried, pushing away from Stacie to face the whole group. "That isn't the way to do things. What happens if Jeremy folds the team? We are so close to our goal. Let's just work it out."

"It's too late for that, Laurie," Stacie said. "Either Lexi goes, or we don't play. Period."

"Here comes Jeremy," Rianne said and the girls turned to face him. Alecia stood awkwardly, not sure where she belonged. Not sure what to do.

Stacie did all the talking. She had obviously thought out ahead of time what she was going to say. Laurie stood with her head down, staring at the ground. Nancy had her arms crossed, her face tight with anger. Jeremy listened until Stacie had finished speaking.

"I see," he said when she had finished. He looked around at his team, meeting everyone's eye. Some of the girls were staring hard at the ground. He came to Alecia and his eyes questioned her. She lowered her head, her face flushing with heat.

"Jeremy, I tried to talk them out of it," Laurie said.

"Don't worry about it, Laurie. This is not your fault."

"It is! It's because I quit as captain," Laurie cried, tears springing to her eyes. "I shouldn't have given up so easily. I should have honoured my commitment. If I agree to be captain again will you change your minds?" she asked, spinning around. Stacie hesitated, then shook her head.

"We won't play with Lexi."

Alecia spotted Lexi across the field, walking slowly, her head down, her bag dragging behind her. Alecia's heart started pounding harder. What would Lexi do when she found out what was going on? Would she agree to go away? Or would she stick her heels in and refuse to back down? Alecia couldn't guess.

"I won't chase a girl from my team," Jeremy told them at last. "If you are sure this is what you want to do," he said slowly, looking at each girl again, "then I will forfeit. You do realize that this game counts for a whole lot? If we win today against the Rocketeers, we are sitting in a perfect position heading for the finals. I want each of you to understand that."

Lexi was getting closer. Alecia could see the puzzled look on her face as she walked. The majority of Burrards nodded their understanding of what they were willing to give up.

"Fine." Jeremy turned and headed to where the referee was standing. He passed Lexi, but said nothing to her, didn't even acknowledge her. Lexi stopped when she got to the team and dropped her bag.

"What is going on now?" she demanded. "Some secret club meeting?"

No one said anything. Jeremy came back a second later and picked up the mesh bag of balls.

"Go on home, then," he said quietly, "there is no game today."

"What do you mean there is no game?" Lexi cried. "What's going on?"

For a long, painful minute no one said anything, but at last Stacie stepped forward and explained. Lexi's face went pale at the words but she said nothing. Her shoulders were slumped, arms hanging by her sides. Her hair, in its sloppy ponytail, had come loose and was blowing about her face as she looked at the girls gathered around.

"I won't be chased away," she said at last. "I have a right to play with this team and I'm going to play."

"Not today, you're not," Stacie snapped at her. Lexi grabbed her bag and ran from the field. Behind her, no one said anything.

★ ★ ★

The air in the car driving home was heavy with emotion. Alecia felt as though she were drowning in it. She wanted to speak, to say something to Jeremy, but there didn't seem to be anything to say. His disappointment felt like lead weights on her shoulders. Did he even like her anymore? What would he do now? Her thoughts were muddled and scattered, jumping from one thing to another.

They were almost home before Jeremy cleared his throat. Alecia braced herself for what he would say. She held tight to the strap of her bag as though it might protect her in some way.

"I won't be blackmailed, Alecia. Do you understand that?" he asked softly, as he pulled the car into the garage. "I won't be forced to kick a girl from my team, not by other players."

"They're angry because Laurie is upset and doesn't want to be captain anymore," Alecia whispered.

"Partly. Partly they just don't like Lexi. I understand that. She's abrasive and bossy and not easy to get along with. Did you ever once, any of you, try to get past that? Did you ever talk to Lexi, any of you? Get to know her? You girls were resistant to her joining from the very first day and when she proved hard to get to know, you just stopped trying altogether."

Jeremy looked over at Alecia for a second, letting her absorb his words. She squirmed under his gaze and stared out the window at the wall of tools, carefully laid out on their board.

"You asked me once what happened to Lexi's mother, why she didn't live with her. Did you ever bother to find out?" he asked.

"No," Alecia muttered, reddening under his gaze.

"Lexi is a good soccer player," Jeremy continued. "She has good instincts and a good eye, plus she's fast and she reads her opponents very well. I think if given a chance, she'd enjoy playing with us. We're a good team, a good match for her, skillwise. But some people aren't easy to get to know. You have to work a little harder with them, push past the walls they put up. And sometimes it's worth the effort."

11 ONE BIG MESS

Alecia hid in her room most of Sunday, miserable and angry and frustrated. She didn't want to face Jeremy, who looked so disappointed and upset every time she caught his eye that she felt like a knife was jabbing into her heart. She knew he didn't hold her personally responsible for the boycott, but she was part of the group. And as part of the group she had not made things any better. The problem was, she had no idea how to fix things. What could she do? Would Lexi even come back? A lot of things would be resolved if Lexi would just quit. But a lot would be left unresolved.

She got next to nothing done as far as homework went and headed off to school Monday morning feeling slightly sick. If she could have gotten away with it, Alecia would have just stayed in her room forever, hiding.

Anne and Monica were waiting for her at their usual corner. Monica full of her usual good cheer and bubbling chatter, Anne anxious and worried.

"I'll tell you when we get to our lockers," Alecia whispered, grabbing Anne's arm as she joined her friends.

"You'll never guess! Never, never, never in a million years will you guess what happened over the weekend!" Monica cried, bursting with her news.

"Then you'd better tell us," Alecia said, pulling herself out of her funk. Monica's chatter was a useful distraction this morning. It made it hard for her tortured thoughts to take hold of her.

"My mom told me she's pregnant! She's having a baby!" she cried, clapping her hands together. Alecia and Anne looked at each other in stunned silence. Monica laughed, throwing her head back. "Isn't that unreal? I'm going to have a little brother or sister. Well, another one. I already have Cam. I am so excited! Mom and Dad are pretty happy. They've been trying for a long time. Years. The doctors kept telling them they couldn't get pregnant, they couldn't have their own kids. It was just killing my mother. I mean, she loves me and Cam, I know that. But she really wanted her own. And here, all these years after I showed up, is another one!"

Alecia frowned, confused. "Are you adopted, Monica?" she asked, hesitantly. It seemed such a personal thing to ask.

Monica gave her a little shove and laughed again, flipping her hair over her shoulder. "Yes! Didn't you girls know that? I thought you knew. Cam and I are both adopted. Mom and Dad tried for years and nothing! Not one silly thing! But then, all of a sudden ... ! Mom is only forty, not very old at all. She figured she was going through menopause, then the doctor told her, nope! It's a baby! She's a little nervous, but she's healthy. She'll be fine. I am so excited!"

Alecia stared hard at the ground. Monica, adopted? Still, it wasn't quite the same thing as her situation. Alecia was nearly fourteen — Monica had been adopted as a baby. But then, she knew Jeremy, had known him for years.

"Do you like being adopted? I mean," she paused, blushing, "do your parents treat you like you were their real, natural daughter?" she asked.

Monica laughed again. Nothing fazed her. "Of course! They are the best. I even look a bit like my dad."

"Still, you were adopted as a baby. You don't even remember anyone else," Alecia said.

"No," Monica told her, some of the bounce going out of her. She spoke more quietly. "Cam and I were adopted eight years ago. I was six. Cam was a baby."

Neither Anne nor Alecia knew what to say to that. Alecia looked at Monica, a new respect growing for the girl. She loved her parents. She called them Mom and Dad. She thought she looked a little like her father, even though he wasn't her natural dad. It was all rather bewildering.

"Our mother died just after Cam was born. Dad

took off, so they put us in foster care. Our foster mother was pretty nice. I don't remember her all that well. We stayed with her until they tracked down our birth father and he gave up his rights to us. Our foster mother didn't want to adopt us, so they found the Jenkins. We've been with them ever since."

"That's amazing, Monica," Anne said softly, smiling at her. "You were so lucky."

"I guess. Man, this conversation is getting so sad and depressing. Let's talk about baby names! I hope it's a girl. I really want a sister!" Monica said. Alecia listened with half an ear as Monica and Anne discussed baby names.

She was stunned by Monica's news. Stunned and a little curious. She had a lot of questions she would have liked to ask, but Monica obviously didn't want to talk about it any more. She was more interested in possible names. Alecia walked along silently, stealing glances at Monica every once in a while. Somehow, the girl seemed like a whole different person to her now.

"So tell me what happened! Was Jeremy really mad?" Anne demanded when they finally said goodbye to Monica and headed for their own lockers. Alecia sighed. Monica's news had completely chased away all thoughts about Lexi and the Burrards. They came flooding back quickly, however.

"It was awful. Stacie just said they wouldn't play if Lexi was allowed to play and Jeremy said he wouldn't be blackmailed into forcing a girl off his team and he forfeited the game. Then he was really disappointed and upset."

"Oh, Alecia! How awful! What is going to happen now?" Anne asked.

"I don't know." Her thoughts were all jumbled and her stomach tied in knots. There had to be a way to resolve this mess, but what was it?

★ ★ ★

"What are we going to do now?" Alecia asked Stacie over the phone. "I mean, you take this big stand, the game is called, but Jeremy won't kick Lexi off the team. So what happens next?"

She had decided, on the way home from school that afternoon, that she needed to talk to Stacie. The boycott had been Stacie's idea in the first place. *She* should fix things now that they were a big mess. At least, as far as Alecia was concerned she should. But Stacie didn't seem to be all that agreeable to the idea.

"What do you mean, 'what happens next?' We said we wouldn't play with Lexi, so we don't play until she leaves the team. We want Laurie back as captain and Lexi gone."

"Jeremy isn't going to do that, Stace," Alecia told her, again. "He says he won't be blackmailed."

"Well, then I guess we don't have a team."

"You're just going to let it all go down the toilet

then? Not play soccer anymore?" Alecia asked, stunned. She hadn't thought Stacie would let it go that far. But then a small thought came to her. Stacie didn't want to back down. She didn't want to be seen as giving in.

"I'll find another team."

"What about the others?" Alecia wanted to know. "Do they agree with you too?"

There was a short silence on the other end of the line. "I don't know, Alecia. Why don't you ask them? I've got stuff to do." Stacie hung up without saying goodbye.

Alecia stared at the phone for a minute. That was it. Stacie didn't want to admit defeat. Jeremy had called her bluff and now she had to quit rather than look foolish.

"Stubborn jerk," Alecia muttered, angrily. She kicked at the innocent shoe lying on the floor beside her mother's bed. Now what? she wondered. She didn't want to have her team fold because of this. It was too stupid a battle. They could figure out a way of playing with Lexi, couldn't they?

She called Laurie next. It was too difficult having all this on her shoulders alone. She needed someone to help her decide what to do. Laurie was the most level-headed person she knew. She would know what to do.

"What do we do now?" Alecia asked, when she'd filled Laurie in on her conversation with Stacie. "Do the others feel the same way?"

"I don't know how the others feel. Well," Laurie corrected herself, "Nancy was against it to begin with. And I think maybe one or two others." She paused and Alecia could hear her breathing, knew she was thinking things through.

"We can't let Stacie decide what's going to happen with our team, Laurie," Alecia said, breaking the silence. "It's not fair. Just because she doesn't like Lexi, doesn't mean she can just ruin everything for the rest of us."

"I know, I know," Laurie agreed. "But maybe it's too late. Maybe it's all too late."

"Will you come back as captain? You said you would last Sunday."

"I know I did. But I just don't know," Laurie said slowly. "I can't fight Lexi all the time. I don't like it. I can't play well when there is so much fighting. I won't leave the team, I promise. But I don't know about being captain."

"Well, that's a good start anyway," Alecia decided. "First we need a team, then we can work on the captain bit. Do we call everyone ahead of tomorrow's practice or do we just show up?"

"Let's just show up. See who is there. See if Lexi shows. Decide when we get there. Is Stacie going to be at practice, do you know?" Laurie asked.

"I don't know. She just hung up. Why don't you call her? She says she's doing all this because of you, wanting you back as captain. She may listen to you."

"That's a good idea. I'll see you tomorrow night, Leesh. Hopefully all this will work out."

Alecia hoped so too. What would she do if it didn't? She couldn't stand the idea of not having the Burrards anymore. Somehow, some way, they had to fix things.

12 FIXING THINGS

"Practice tonight, Leesh," Jeremy reminded her the next morning.

"Yeah, I know," she muttered into her cereal. They hadn't said an awful lot to each other in the last couple of days.

"What am I going to walk into?" her stepfather asked. Alecia looked up at him. He was wearing a suit and tie that morning, and the tie did not have any cartoon characters on it. He has a meeting today, Alecia thought to herself. It was funny how she could always tell what kind of day Jeremy had planned by the way he looked in the morning. He knew her too. Knew when she had a test or a project due by the way she sat hunched over her breakfast and refused to laugh at his lame jokes. They knew each other well, she thought, pleased by the realization.

"I don't know, Jeremy," she told him honestly. "I really don't know."

He got up and put his breakfast dishes in the dishwasher. As he picked up his briefcase he glanced at her, his eyes serious. "I heard you talking to Laurie last night," he said.

"Yeah, I talked to Laurie, but talking about it with Laurie isn't solving the problem, is it?" Alecia snapped.

Jeremy ignored her tone and continued to look at her until Alecia started to squirm. "Have you thought about confronting Lexi?" he asked at last. Alecia closed her eyes and shook her head.

"What good would that do?" she asked. "It would just be a big shouting match, with her telling me to mind my own business, as usual. Then she'd go storming off and nothing would be any different than it is now. And why should I be the one to do it? Seems to me it's the captain's job to deal with this kind of thing."

"At the moment you don't have a captain, do you?" Jeremy asked. "And maybe she would react that way," he went on. "But on the other hand, she might talk to you, if you asked the right questions."

Her voice barely a whisper, Alecia asked, "What questions would those be?"

Jeremy smiled at her and opened the door to the garage. "I think, my dear, that you know what they are. I'll see you tonight. Have a good day," he said, leaving Alecia alone in the silent kitchen.

★ ★ ★

"How long will Laurie be with her tutoring?" Alecia asked, hunting through her locker for the piece of music she needed. Connor leaned against Anne's locker, his arms folded across his chest.

"She said it would only be a half-hour or so," he told her. "I promised I'd wait this time. She's been pretty upset lately."

"Yeah, I know," Alecia muttered. She found what she was looking for and stood up, holding it out triumphantly. "Well, I guess that's it. I'll see you tomorrow."

"You haven't talked to Lexi yet," he reminded her.

Alecia scowled at him. She hadn't forgotten, she was just hoping that she had missed her. "I haven't seen Lexi all day," she said.

She had confided in Connor that morning, needing to talk to someone about it. He thought it was worth a try and had even given her some suggestions of things she might say. Hopefully Alecia would remember them when the time came.

"Well, don't decide not to do it," he warned her, looking stern. "Even when she's nasty and says things that bug you."

"Yes, sir," Alecia said, swinging her backpack onto her shoulders. "I'll see you later."

She pushed open the orange fire door and stepped outside into the winter afternoon. She frowned at the figure seated on the cement steps, leaning against the chipped metal handrail. It was Lexi. Alecia's heart pounded and her mouth went dry.

The girl didn't turn around as Alecia came up behind her and sat down on the steps. The cement was cold and slightly damp and Alecia shifted uncomfortably. Lexi turned then and glanced at her, her characteristic scowl firmly in place. She said nothing, but turned away again a second later and stared off over the empty schoolyard.

"What do you want?" she asked at last.

"Well," Alecia said slowly, gathering her thoughts together. "I was hoping I could talk to you about Sunday and about the team and stuff."

Lexi snorted and shook her head. She stared down at her hands, playing with the strap of her backpack. "What is there to talk about, *Leesh*? Stacie made it all perfectly clear you guys don't want me on the team."

"You know," Alecia said slowly, "part of the reason they don't want you on the team is because you're always so rude. Maybe if you would just be a tiny bit less bossy and nasty, the other girls would be more welcoming. They don't all think like Stacie."

"You guys didn't want me there from the first practice!" Lexi cried. "You think I didn't know that? You were all perfect just the way you were. Perfect coach, perfect captain, perfect goalkeeper! You looked at me like I was an intruder. You make me sick!" Lexi stared at the ground, her hands balled into fists in her lap. Her hair fell over her face and her shoulders heaved.

"Then why do you keep coming to play, if you hate us all so much? If you don't think we want you anyway?" Alecia asked. She watched Lexi struggle not to cry.

"Where else am I supposed to go?" Lexi's head snapped up as she spoke and she glared at Alecia. "My dad doesn't want me around. He'll just find another team for me to play on, and another, and another. Anything to keep me out of his way." Her voice rose with each word until she was yelling at Alecia.

Alecia thought of the overheard conversations and of the little scene at the soccer game a few weeks back. Things were beginning to make more sense. She stared at Lexi, unsure what to say. She had never been very good at this kind of thing. She wished desperately that Annie was with her. Annie would know what to do, what to say. But she was alone. And it was up to her to fix things, to get things back the way they'd been before.

"Can't you live with your mother?" she asked, innocently.

"My mother's dead. She died a year and a half ago. I have nowhere else to go." There was no emotion behind the words, just cold fact. Alecia blinked, stunned. She hadn't expected that.

"I'm so sorry, Lexi," she whispered. "That's terrible."

The two girls sat silently, Lexi staring across the school yard, Alecia staring at Lexi. She felt a huge knot in her chest and her eyes stung with tears. "My dad died, too, you know," she confessed at last.

Lexi's head shot up and she frowned at Alecia. "What do you mean? Jeremy's your dad," she said.

"No, not Jeremy. He's my stepfather. I mean my real dad. He died when I was four." They had something in common, she and Lexi, Alecia thought. But Lexi didn't look at it that way.

"When you were four? You probably can't even remember him. Jeremy's your dad. He's the one who cheers you on at games, who pats you on the back when you make a good play."

"Yeah, he does. But he's not my father... not my *real* father," Alecia insisted.

Lexi shook her head, her eyes scornful. "Real father?" she repeated. "You don't even know what a real father is. You've got this perfect little family sitting right there and you don't even know it."

Alecia started to defend herself, defend her dead father and the place he had in her life when Lexi made a rude noise. "I'm going home," she said, grabbing her bag. Alecia struggled for something to say that would stop her leaving, but nothing came to her and in another second Lexi had disappeared.

★ ★ ★

That night, Alecia and Jeremy came into the gym for practice to find everyone already there, sitting on the floor. Everyone but Lexi, that is. Alecia's heart beat harder and her hands grew clammy. Would Lexi show up tonight? Would she come back? She had said if she didn't play on this team her dad would just find another one for her. Alecia shivered, what an awful reason to play a game. Still, Lexi had chosen soccer and she was good at it. She just needed to find the right team. And maybe the Burrards were that team. Maybe.

"Well," Jeremy said, glancing around at everyone, "since we're mostly all here, why don't we get started on our warm-up. We have a lot to do." Jeremy went off to a corner to set up the cones for drills and the girls slowly got up and started running around the gym.

They were stretching when Lexi arrived. She glared around the gym defiantly, as though daring the others to tell her to leave. But Alecia caught the trembling in her hands as she took off her jacket and slipped on her shin pads. She was pale, too, and her eyes were red-rimmed. Alecia cleared her throat, then turned, concentrating on her leg stretches.

Jeremy gave them their drills and told them to get busy. But only a few of the girls got to their feet. Some looked hesitantly at Stacie. Some looked at Laurie. Most looked at the floor.

"We won't play if Lexi is on the team," Stacie reminded Jeremy. She was standing, hands on her hips, her face hard and unfriendly. Alecia looked away.

"Is this the way you all feel?" Jeremy asked. About two-thirds of the team nodded. Reluctantly, Alecia thought. "I had thought that the weekend would have given you enough time to think things through. Realize the mistake you're making. You see," he said slowly, looking at each girl in turn, "I don't work this way. I won't be blackmailed. I won't force a girl from my team unless there is a very, very good reason. And I don't think there is one in this case."

"You know what, Jeremy?" Lexi said, speaking in a loud, clear voice. "I don't want this anyway. I'll just leave. You can have your stupid team." She moved to the bench to pick up her things, her head bent, defeated. Alecia looked around at her teammates, at their sullen, silent faces. She thought of the way they had pushed Lexi away from the very beginning. All of them wanting Annie back, not some stranger with an attitude. She thought of the confession Lexi had made about her dad and not being wanted. Alecia had been wanted her whole life. What must it be like to not feel wanted anywhere, even at home? She took a deep breath and let it out slowly. Suddenly she knew what she had to do.

"Wait, Lexi," she called, jumping up and running after the girl. "Don't leave. Please."

Lexi dropped her jacket onto the bench and stared at Alecia. "Why not? You guys don't want me here. You've made that pretty clear."

"You're right, we didn't want you at first," Alecia told her. "But that doesn't mean we can't change our minds. Look, we weren't very nice when you first joined the team. I'm sorry about that. We should have been more welcoming. Jeremy told us to give you a chance and we didn't. But we want you to give us a second chance now. Please. We need you on our team. We've just been kind of slow to realize it. We want you to stay."

"Who's we?" Lexi demanded, her voice still tight and angry, but some of the fight going out of her eyes.

"Me," Laurie said, joining Alecia. Alecia smiled, but held her breath. Who else?

"And me," Nancy and Rianne said together. They came and stood beside Laurie.

"Us too," Marnie said as she and Allison moved over as well. In groups of two and three the others joined Alecia and Laurie. Soon Stacie was standing alone.

Alecia looked over at her, frowning. "Stacie, won't you give Lexi another chance? We need you too," she said. She was amazed at how everyone had followed her lead. Amazed and thrilled. She had done it! Well, almost. Stacie was still glaring at them all.

"I said I wouldn't play with Lexi on the team and I'm not going to. I'm out of here," she said and in another second the door closed behind her. For a minute no one said anything, just stared at the closed door. Finally Jeremy cleared his throat.

"Well," he said, breaking the silence, "since we still have a soccer team, perhaps we should hold a practice." He sent the girls off to do drills, calling out directions as they spread out around the gym.

Slowly Alecia followed along, watching as the little groups of two and three formed. She didn't for a second believe that their problems were completely solved, but they were working on it and that was a good start. She caught Lexi's eye and grinned at her and, amazingly, Lexi smiled back.

13 ALECIA DECIDES

"So everything worked out okay, then?" Anne asked Wednesday morning.

"Yes, sort of," Alecia told her, thinking of Stacie's abrupt departure from the team. "Stacie refused to stay, but we're hoping Laurie can work on her, convince her to come back. Karen will be good as goalkeeper, but we want Stacie back."

"Maybe Stacie just needs time to cool off," Anne said, but didn't sound too convinced. "Stacie's always been kind of hotheaded about things."

"At least Laurie agreed to be captain again. It took some convincing, though. She didn't want to do it," Alecia said.

"Well," Anne said, sighing. "I'm glad all that is settled. It will be easier to get on with things now, right? No more tension and fighting at practices? And the playoffs are getting so close! You guys have to work hard to get a good position."

"I'm sure Lexi hasn't become Miss Mary Sunshine

or anything. She'll probably still annoy everyone. Still, I think we'll be okay," Alecia agreed. It was great that the Burrards had sorted themselves out, finally. A huge weight had been lifted from Alecia's shoulders.

"Wasn't that amazing what Monica told us yesterday?" Anne asked, a second later. Monica hadn't been at the corner that morning. Anne didn't know where she was. "She never told me that before. Although I guess there was never any reason why she would. It is kind of personal, after all."

Alecia didn't answer. Soccer might be all sorted out, but there were other things that hadn't been decided. Decisions she hadn't been able to make. She knew Jeremy wouldn't want to wait for her answer forever.

"Do you think Jeremy would ever adopt you, Leesh?" Anne asked, startling Alecia so much she tripped over a crack in the sidewalk and nearly ended up on the ground. Anne grabbed her arm to steady her. "Are you okay?" she asked.

"Yeah," Alecia told her, hoping Anne would forget her question. No such luck, however.

"Do you think he would adopt you? I wonder about that sometimes. You must too," Anne said, looking thoughtful. "It would be so great for you to have a real dad again. To have a real and true family."

"We *are* a real and true family," Alecia said, a little snappishly.

"Oh I know you are, Alecia, I didn't mean anything

by that. Just that you aren't Jeremy's daughter legally. Don't you think about it?"

She'd thought about talking to Anne about the whole thing many times, but hadn't ever gotten up the nerve. "The thing is, Annie," Alecia said, jumping in with both feet, "he has already asked."

"No way! Why didn't you say anything before? That is the best news ever!" Anne cried, throwing her arms around Alecia.

"Annie, wait," she said, peeling her friend's arms off her. "I haven't told him yes yet."

Anne frowned at her. "Why not? What are you waiting for?" she asked.

"I can't decide. I mean, what about my own dad?" Alecia said softly. It was hard for her to talk about.

"What do you mean? He's dead, Leesh. You don't even remember him," Anne said. "Jeremy is here. He's great. You love him. He loves you. I think it's wonderful."

Why didn't Alecia think so? Why was she clinging so hard to the memory of her dead father? "Yeah, I guess," she agreed. She wished suddenly that she hadn't brought it up with Anne. Anne was a good friend, one or her best friends, but she didn't understand. No one really understood.

"Well, I think you should say yes. But anyway, it's your decision. I wonder if Mr. Ellison remembered we're supposed to have a quiz in science today. I sure hope he forgot. I didn't understand much of the chapter,"

Anne said, changing the subject. Alecia listened with one ear as Anne talked. She wished it was as easy as Anne seemed to think it was.

★ ★ ★

When she got home that afternoon she went straight to her room and pulled out the scrapbook. She flipped through the pages slowly, the scent of English Navy after-shave wafting up with each page she turned. Her father's life appeared before her, all laid out carefully, from his baby pictures, to school pictures, to team photos. There was also the graduation photo she had secretly taken away earlier and a wedding picture. Alecia touched the pictures gently with her fingertips. Her grandmother had surprised her with a whole box of things one day when they had been visiting. Alecia had carefully picked through the mementos, choosing the things that spoke to her the most. Today, however, they said nothing. They just sat on the page. It could have been anyone's father staring back at her from the plastic-covered pages for all the memory they evoked.

Alecia's throat thickened and her eyes burned. What had she expected? she asked herself, angry. That he would suddenly speak to her from the great beyond? She was so stupid! She pushed the scrapbook and it slid to the floor, landing with a thud on the throw rug. She threw herself down and cried into her pillow. She cried for a long, long time.

"Alecia?" her mother asked from the doorway. Alecia hadn't heard her come home, hadn't heard anything but the roaring in her head and her own sobs. "Alecia, sweetheart, are you all right?" Mrs. Parker asked.

Alecia rolled over and blinked, watching as her mother crossed the room and sat beside her on the bed. "What's all this about?" she asked, smoothing the hair back from Alecia's face with gentle fingers. Alecia sat up and leaned against the headboard. She said nothing.

"You knocked a book on the floor," her mother said leaning down to retrieve it. She brought it up slowly, frowning at the words printed on the inside of the cover. "What's this?" she asked, glancing at Alecia.

Alecia reached for it, wanting to prevent her mother from seeing anything more, but it was too late. She drew her knees up and hid her face in her arms, embarrassed and ashamed and hating her mother for coming in. There was no sound at all in the room but the gentle swish of pages being turned and the scent of English Navy in the air around them.

"Alecia?" her mother said at last, touching her arm. "Sweetie, look at me."

Alecia forced herself to look up and was amazed at what she saw. Her mother had tears in her eyes. "Would you like to tell me about this?" she asked gently, wiping the tears away with one hand. Alecia had not intended to talk to anyone about this, not ever. But her mother's soft voice and gentle caresses opened her mouth.

Once Alecia started to talk, the words seemed to flow from her like a river. She told her mother about the ad on TV, about the talk she'd had with Connor, about looking at the pictures. She told her about feeling left out when Anne and Monica were talking about their dads or when Connor described yet another adventure he and Mr. Stevens had gone on.

"I wanted my dad," she confessed at last, sniffling. "Everyone else has their dad. I felt left out."

Mrs. Parker pulled Alecia close to her and held her tightly. "Has this helped? This scrapbook?" she asked softly.

Alecia shook her head against her mother's shoulder. "No," she mumbled. "I had hoped it would help me remember something about him. Remember something that no one had ever told me or shown me in a picture. But it didn't. I don't remember him at all. I don't know who he was."

"Do you know why collecting these things hasn't helped you know your dad?" Mrs. Parker asked. "They're just objects, Leesh. Objects don't define a person. Your father's report card and his favourite blanket are just objects he owned. Just like your old bear doesn't tell me who you are.

"I can't give you your father, Alecia. He's been gone a long time. And I'm sorry. I'm sorry every day that you didn't get to know what a wonderful person he was, how loving and gentle and kind he was. I hate that you never knew how much he loved you and wanted to watch you grow up to be this beautiful young woman. But I can't change any of that." Mrs. Parker kissed the top of Alecia's head, burying her face in her hair. They sat silently for a long time.

Eventually she pulled away from Alecia and tilted her face to look at her. "But you do have a father, you know," she said softly.

"Jeremy."

"Yes, Jeremy. Do you know how much he loves you? How proud he is of you? You're a very lucky girl."

"I know," Alecia whispered.

"Do you? I don't know if you really, really know how lucky you are. Bringing a child into this world doesn't mean a thing, Leesh. It's what you do with that child once it is here that counts. Any man can be a father, but it takes someone special to be a dad."

Alecia thought of the things Lexi had said the other day, accusing her of not knowing how good she had it. Lexi lived with her biological father, but he wasn't much of one to her. And Monica, adopted by a man she thought was the greatest thing in the world. Still, Alecia struggled.

"I don't want to betray my own father," she whispered, leaning against her mother.

"Sweetie, you betray him when you don't get on with your life. Do you think he wanted us to be alone the rest of our lives? You don't think my marrying Jeremy betrays Peter, do you? No, of course not. He wanted us to be happy. I think he'd be very pleased with the choice we made."

"I didn't choose Jeremy," Alecia said, pulling back to look at her mother. "You did."

"No, I didn't, not by myself. If you hadn't liked him, we would never have had a second date. You may not remember this, but when Jeremy came to our apartment the first time, you climbed right up into his lap and demanded he read a book to you. He was completely stunned, but he read the book. Three times."

She didn't remember doing that, but she did have a lifetime of memories that included Jeremy: swimming at the lake, learning to ride a bike, picnics at Stanley Park. He had taken her to her first day of school because her mother was sick and had held her hand until she was ready for him to leave. Things were becoming clearer to Alecia, slowly but surely.

Her mother kissed her forehead and hugged her tightly. "If you want to know who your father was, ask me. I will always answer your questions if I can. And if I don't know the answer, I'll help you find out."

"Okay, I promise," Alecia told her. She sat up and wiped her hair out of her eyes.

"I'm going to go change and then we'll make some dinner. Are you okay now?" her mother asked, standing. Alecia nodded, smiling.

"Is it okay if I keep my scrapbook, though?" she asked, touching the glossy cover. Her mother laughed, nodding.

"Of course! I should have made one for you years ago. I think it is a nice idea. And I think I may have some more things you can put in it."

After her mother left, Alecia sat on the bed by herself, her thoughts swirling around in her head, all jumbled and confused. She had been looking for her father, but had she been looking in the wrong place all this time? Chasing memories of Peter Sheffield had left Alecia feeling frustrated and lonely. He had been gone a long time. And, if Alecia was truthful with herself, she knew he could never give her what she wanted and needed — a dad. She wanted a dad like Monica's, Annie's, and Connor's, someone who loved her and did things with her and helped her with her problems.

She realized, all of a sudden, how right Lexi had been. Alecia had a wonderful dad who was all those things to her and had been for a long time. She had been so intent on building a dream daddy she had lost sight of the real one. The one who was still, patiently, waiting for her to make a decision. Alecia thought of how much Lexi wanted what Alecia had always taken for granted, and she felt sorry for her. She hoped they could work things out somehow. It was time, however, that she had a chat with Jeremy. But first she had one last thing to take care of.

Dear Peter,

I'm sorry I didn't get to know you before you died. I think I would have liked you a lot. But I have to move on now. You see, Mom did a really good job of picking a new dad for me and I think I'm going to let him adopt me. I know you won't mind. I know you want me to be happy. If you don't mind, though, I might still write to you sometimes — you know, when I need to think things through.

Love, Alecia

Jeremy was in the garage, puttering with his tool bench. Alecia stood in the doorway watching him, a small smile playing at her lips. He was so funny, the way he muttered to himself, even argued once in a while. He reached up and scratched his nose with one finger, frowning as he looked around the untidy bench.

"Lose something?" Alecia asked. Jeremy turned and smiled at her. He gave a small laugh and glanced back at the tool bench.

"Who'd think it possible, eh? I mean this is such a tidy and organized place."

"What are you looking for?" Alecia asked, moving into the room. She came and stood beside him by the bench, pretending to hunt for whatever it was he needed.

"It's called a thingamajig and it is a highly advanced

piece of equipment. Only a few people in the world know how to use one," Jeremy told her, dropping one arm over Alecia's shoulder. She pressed in close to him, liking the solid strength of him near her.

"I thought you might be looking for a daughter," she whispered. There was a short pause.

"Would you happen to know where I could find one?" he asked at last, his voice catching, just a little.

"I'm available," Alecia told him. Jeremy turned so they were facing each other, his hands holding her shoulders. She looked up and met his eyes, her own suddenly brimming with tears. "That is, if you're still interested," she added.

"Oh I'm definitely still interested," Jeremy said and pulled her tightly against him. Alecia wrapped her arms around his waist and held on tight.

"I'm sorry it took me so long to decide," she whispered against the soft cotton of his shirt. "I had some things to figure out."

Jeremy hugged her again, laughing softly. "That's okay, some things are worth waiting for."

★ ★ ★

The game Sunday promised to be a good one. Jeremy had spoken to the Rocketeers' coach and to the league officials and explained what had happened with the Burrards and surprisingly, everyone had agreed to reschedule the game. Alecia woke up that morning feeling as light as a feather. She felt like she could score every goal single-handedly, make every check on every player, do anything!

Everyone but Stacie was on the field ready to go when Jeremy, Alecia, and her mother arrived Sunday morning. Laurie had not been able to convince Stacie to come back. Alecia still held out hope that they would convince her, eventually, but she also realized Stacie was pretty stubborn. And in the meantime they had Karen, who was just waiting to be needed to give the team her best.

"Hey, guys," Alecia called joining her teammates at their bench. "Isn't it a gorgeous day? It feels almost like spring."

"Please, Alecia," Allison grumbled, "it is way too early in the morning for so much cheer. Besides, spring is a month away. And it's cold."

"Never mind her," Laurie said, laughing. "It does feel good today. And look who came to watch!" Alecia turned to see Connor, Monica, Anne, and some boy Alecia didn't recognize walking toward them. Monica waved.

"What got you out of bed so early on a Sunday morning?" Laurie asked as the group approached.

"Well, Trevor here wanted to see your game. He plays too," Connor said, pointing to his friend. The tall boy with sandy hair and glasses that kept slipping down his nose grinned shyly at the girls. Alecia felt herself blushing when he caught her eye and smiled at her. She tossed her head and looked away, suddenly very self-conscious.

"Aren't you going to introduce us?" Laurie said, poking Connor in the ribs. "He is so rude," she told Trevor. Trevor laughed shyly.

"Trevor Lunden," Connor said, putting on his polite voice, "these are my friends, Laurie Chen and Alecia Sheffield."

Alecia smiled, but shook her head. "Actually," she said, speaking clearly, "it's Parker," she told them, turning to catch Jeremy's eye. He winked at her, smiling, and Alecia laughed.

"It's Alecia Parker," she said again and found she liked the sound of it.

MORE SPORTS, MORE ACTION
www.lorimer.ca

CHECK OUT THESE OTHER SOCCER STORIES FROM LORIMER'S SPORTS STORIES SERIES:

Alecia's Challenge
by Sandra Diersch

Getting used to a new school and a new stepfather is bad enough, then suddenly Alecia's best friend quits the soccer team. Alecia only joined the team to be with Anne — she doesn't even *like* soccer — but now her stepdad won't let her quit!

Play On
by Sandra Diersch

Alecia's soccer team has made it to the top of the league, and things finally seem to be looking up. But then a vicious piece of gossip and old rivalries threaten to tear her team apart. Can they get it together in time for the finals?

Corner Kick
by Bill Swan

Michael Strike's the most popular guy in school and the most talented soccer player around. But then a new kid from Afghanistan arrives who can show him up on the field, and threatens to steal his spotlight . . .

LORIMER

Falling Star
by Robert Rayner

He's super-talented on the pitch, but lately Edison seems to have lost his nerve. He hesitates and misses shot after shot. Can a ragtag group of soccer misfits show him what the game is really about before it's too late?

Foul Play
by Beverly Scudamore

When her team's chance at winning a tournament is foiled by freshly-dug holes in their practice field, Remy gets suspicious. Is someone trying to sabotage them? She'll bet everything that the captain of the rival team — her ex-best friend — is behind it.

Just for Kicks
by Robert Rayner

Toby's not the greatest or most athletic player on the field, but he sure loves to play. But when new coaches arrive and try to organize the pickup soccer players into a league, it doesn't matter who's friend, foe, or family — it only matters who wins.

Soccer Showdown
by John Danakas

Lizzie's just been named captain of the soccer team — the *boys'* soccer team — but some of her teammates aren't playing nice. Will it be boys vs. girls forever, or can Lizzie think of a way to settle the score, once and for all?

Little's Losers
by Robert Rayner

The Brunswick Valley soccer team isn't just bad — they're terrible. The worst. So awful, in fact, that their coach gives up and quits. No one is more surprised than they are when they make it to the playoffs, but who will coach them now?

Off the Wall
by Camilla Reghelini Rivers

Soccer is the one thing Lizzie Lucas can look forward to when nothing else seems to be going her way. But then her perfect little sister, who outshines her at everything, decides she wants to play too . . . in the same league.

Out of Sight
by Robert Rayner

Lately, the star goalkeeper on Linh-Mai's team has been acting a little strange — missing easy saves, passing to the wrong teammates, not noticing Linh-Mai's new glasses . . . Linh-Mai thinks he might need glasses of his own, but the problem may turn out to be more serious.

Soccer Star
by Jacqueline Guest

Sam has spent her whole life moving from place to place. But now she feels like she doesn't know who she really is or where she belongs. In order to "find herself," Sam has a habit of signing up for too many activities at once. But can she be a star at everything?

Suspended
by Robert Rayner

There's a new principal at Brunswick Valley School, and the establishment is out to shut down the soccer team. For team captain Shay Sutton, the only way to fight fire is with fire, and he enlists the aid of two high school thugs to help them out.

Trading Goals
by Trevor Kew

Vicky lives for soccer, and dreams of being on the national team. But when she suddenly has to switch schools, she finds herself on the same team as her fiercest rival, a goalkeeper named Britney — and there's only room for one girl in the net.

Trapped
by Michele Martin Bossley

Nothing seems to be going right for Jane's soccer team this season. Then some of the girls' stuff starts going missing. Everyone points the finger at the new girl, but Jane is determined to find the *real* culprit . . . and get her team back on track.

Sidelined
by Trevor Kew

Vicky's select soccer team is bound for a tournament in England — the chance of a lifetime! But when a rivalry with her teammate erupts and competition for a guy's interest drives two friends apart, Vicky learns that no one is truly invincible.